About the Author

There was a time when Fiona Dunbar wanted to be a fashion designer...but then she remembered she hated sewing, so she settled for illustration instead. Her first foray into children's fiction was with picture books, which she wrote and illustrated. It was reading to her children that inspired her to try her hand at longer fiction, and her brilliantly successful *Lulu Baker* trilogy proved she was a star on the rise.

Blue Gene Baby is the fantastic second novel in the *Silk Sisters* trilogy, which began with the hugely popular *Pink Chameleon*. Fiona lives in London with her husband and two children.

Praise for *Pink Chameleon*:

'Brilliant fun!'

Mizz

Praise for the *Lulu Baker* t

'Devour the magic – hilarious and absorbing.

Irish Independent

'A deliciously enchanting modern-day fairy tale.'

Books etc

For Siobhan

fiona dunbar

The Silk Sisters

BLUE
gene baby

ORCHARD

Many thanks to Billy Blain for the free sailing lessons, and for so
comprehensively answering all my annoying emails on the subject
when he was trying to get some work done. Thanks also to my
son's headmistress' daughter-in-law, Zita Morris, for giving me the
flying cadet's equivalent of CliffsNotes, only vitamin enriched.
Thanks again to Lee Weatherly (I owe you at this point, Lee!) for
her usual insights, and to Claire Cox for all the information on
hypnosis. Thanks to Ann-Janine and Alice – and thanks to Kirsty
Skidmore and Sarah Lilly for trying so hard to understand how on
earth my mind works, having come to this at such a late stage.

ORCHARD BOOKS
338 Euston Road, London NW1 3BH
Orchard Books Australia
Level 17/207 Kent Street, Sydney NSW 2000

ISBN 978 1 84616 231 2

Typeset by SX Composing DTP, Rayleigh, Essex
Printed in Great Britain.

The paper and board used in this paperback are natural recyclable products made
from wood grown in sustainable forests. The manufacturing processes conform to
the environmental regulations of the country of origin.

Orchard Books is a division of Hachette Children's Books,
an Hachette UK company.
www.hachette.co.uk

'In the future everyone will be world-famous for 15 minutes.'

Andy Warhol

❀

'I'm bored with that line. I never use it any more. My new line is "In 15 minutes everybody will be famous."'

Andy Warhol

❀

'In the future, every 15-year-old will be famous for one minute.'

Anon

❀

Contents

A Note From The Author

At the age of eight, I badly wanted to be Julie Andrews. Specifically, I wanted to be Julie-Andrews-as-Mary-Poppins: beautiful, taking no nonsense from anyone. She could do magic, but it was always in such a nonchalant way (whoops! I've just pulled the contents of an entire room out of my carpetbag!). She knew she was 'practically perfect in every way'; I was anything but.

I never succeeded in becoming Julie Andrews. In any case, I eventually went off the idea of being her, and wanted to be someone else instead – probably a Charlie's Angel. I suppose it won't be long before people will literally be able to try out 'being' their favourite celebrity for a day, a week or a year, using some sort of computer program...there's a story in there somewhere.

This is not that story. It is a different story (dare I say it, an even more exciting one!) that takes place at just around that time. In other words, very soon...

Prologue

'You think long and hard enough about a problem, there's always an answer,' Dad had said. 'Like, way back when people thought, wouldn't it be amazing to go to the moon? Well, they figured out a way to do it, didn't they?'

'But aren't lots of other people thinking long and hard about the same problems as you, and *not* finding the answer?' Rorie remembered asking.

Dad shrugged. 'The way I work is different. I get a *hunch* about something, like a glimpse of a butterfly, and I have to follow it – I just *have* to, I'd go crazy if I didn't.'

'And some people think you're crazy if you *do*,' Mum remarked.

Dad nodded furiously. 'Oh yes. And sometimes you can't see the butterfly for a while, and you search and search. Then, *pop!* there it is again. And this time you're closer, and can see it more clearly...'

'Do people think *you're* crazy, Dad?'
'*Some* people...'

This conversation frequently replayed itself in Rorie's mind; she found it comforting to think that any problem – any problem at all – had a solution, and resolved to believe it, no matter what. And now that Mum and Dad had gone missing – the biggest problem imaginable – she was in great need of the comfort that belief gave her.

Chapter 1
Welcome to Fashionworld

There was just clear, white space in every direction. All around them, brightly coloured 3D blocks hung suspended in the air, rotating slowly. Then the blocks began to spin faster and faster, until they flew together and merged, forming the huge head of an elegant woman in a fancy hat. Her eyes were closed to start with, then they opened. 'Welcome to Fashionworld,' she said in a soft voice that gently reverberated around them.

Next, the woman's head dissolved into a massive red handbag, the size of a small house. It up-ended itself, turning so that its opening was facing them. Then it unfastened, and opened up concertina-style to reveal four sections. Suspended in each section was an oversized version of an object that you might find in a handbag: a packet of gum, a mobile phone, a lipstick and a ticket.

Elsie ran up to the giant chewing-gum packet; on it was the word 'Tribes'. 'Hey, what do you think goes on in here?'

'Let's find out,' said Rorie. She touched the gum, and they found themselves on a city street at night. A sign read 'Choose Your Tribe'; below it indicated the way to places like 'Bohemian Lane' and 'The Cemetery'. On one side of the street, a couple pulled up in a 1950s-style pink Cadillac outside a café where people were jiving to the jukebox. Across the street was a much darker, grungier-looking dive, where people milled around with spiky mohawk haircuts, wearing clothing held together with safety pins.

'Oh, I get it,' said Rorie. 'This is where you try out belonging to different tribes, like rockers over there, and punks over there. If you follow those signs, they lead you to other tribes.'

'Ooh, can I be a Cyber Gypsy?' cried Elsie.

Rorie smiled. 'I guess.' She studied the street sign. 'That's probably...somewhere between "The Space Station" and "Bohemian Lane". Off you go – I'm going to check out "Harajuku Street".'

Elsie trotted off eagerly. Rorie made her way to Harajuku Street; immediately she found herself clad in the frills and furbelows of the 'Gothloli' tribe, blending in with the others around her – who, of course, were not real. She passed her hand right through the middle of a girl nearby, just because she could. She skipped along and twirled around; the theatrical outfit made her feel wonderfully exotic, and sophisticated beyond her twelve years. How nice it was to be transformed in such a frivolous way, for no particular reason – especially after some of the other changes she'd been through lately. Ever since a certain incident, clothing could sometimes have a very peculiar effect on Rorie...

After a while she decided to check in on Elsie, but got waylaid in the spooky night-time darkness of The Cemetery, where Goths mingled with Emos and Psychobillies. She hurried on through, not comfortable with all the blackness that enveloped her. Emerging at last into the bright sunshine of Carnival Street, she found herself in turquoise hotpants and a bright-pink afro wig. She bobbed along with the rest of the virtual revellers until she came to Bohemian Lane, a dirt track alongside a field, where smiling people wafted around in flowing robes. In the middle of the field was a spacecraft painted with flowers; Rorie headed for this, and found Elsie, looking tiny among her much older companions, dressed in the typical Cyber Gypsy jumble of mismatched recycled items.

'OK, I'm done with the tribes,' said Rorie, now clad in a similar outfit. 'Let's find out what else there is.'

Elsie pouted. 'But I wanna stay here with these dudes!'

Rorie laughed. 'Don't be daft, Else. These "dudes" aren't real. Come on – don't you want to see what's in the other sections?'

Elsie considered this. 'OK.'

Together they tried the mobile phone section of the giant virtual handbag, which took them to the world of the Celebrity Paper Doll. Elsie was ecstatic: a vast hall filled with virtual 3D models of stars, each with a wide range of outfits she could dress them in. Heaven for a fashion-obsessed seven-year-old. While she flitted from one model to another, kitting them out in her favourite outfits, Rorie amused herself by dressing Roma Carlton, the celebutante she loved to hate, in the silliest, most unflattering outfits possible.

Elsie was so bowled over by the Lipstick section, she was practically in tears: this was where she got to design and 'make' her own fantasy garments. She created an outrageous jewel-encrusted princess dress. Rorie, on the other hand, spent the whole time customising a pair of slants[1]. Five years older than Elsie, dressing up for her was less about being a princess than just being Rorie Silk – whoever that was.

Then everything around them gradually dissolved, breaking up into millions of pixels and scattering in all directions.

'OK, time's up!' came Nolita's voice from somewhere. 'But don't get up yet; you'll fall over.'

'O-oh! I wanna go back!' wailed Elsie, as the black-glass hood slid up and away from her head. Both she and Rorie were half-reclined in large white circular armchairs.

Blinking as her eyes adjusted to the dimly lit room, Rorie understood how Elsie felt. It wasn't that she cared about Fashionworld particularly; it was just that it was far and away the easiest place to forget all her troubles...

Nolita was standing over them. Today her cherry-red

1. People no longer wear jeans if they want to be comfortable: they wear slants. Abbreviated from 'slouch-pants', they're a dark purply-red and made from a kind of fabric originally devised for Mars miners.

hair was in a short, sleek bob, and she was wearing a close-fitting cream-coloured all-in-one suit with matching cream patent-leather boots. She gave Elsie a diamond-sparkled grin and ruffled her hair. 'Never mind, hon. You can go back real soon,' she said in her punchy, upbeat New York accent. 'That was quite long enough for the first time. How do you feel?'

Well, I'm in the real world again, Rorie wanted to say. *The one where my mum and dad are still missing. How do you think I feel?* But instead she just said, 'Weird. Kind of like I just got off an escalator, only times a hundred.'

'No, it's like rolling down a hill, then standing up,' added Elsie.

Nolita chuckled. 'Well, when you're ready, we'll continue the tour of the house.'

And what a house! To think that not even three weeks ago Uncle Harris had been showing her and Elsie around Poker Bute Hall, the boarding school where he was headmaster. Two weeks' boarding at that awful place, with its 'one correct way' and its sinister 'Perfects' in charge, had felt like an eternity. It was now nineteen days since the event that had prompted it all: the disappearance of Mum and Dad. And now here they were, being shown round yet another new home. But this one was worlds away from Poker Bute Hall. It was as if their lives were plain line-drawings that had just been coloured in with fluorescent gel-pens.

Twenty-four hours ago, Nolita Newbuck, undisputed queen of the fashion world, didn't even know Rorie and Elsie existed. Now, thanks to Elsie's characteristically brazen idea of stowing themselves away in one of her delivery vans, she was not only their legal guardian, but had taken Rorie on as her new Young Teen Model. How on earth did that happen? Rorie still couldn't quite believe it. She half expected all this to disappear into darkness; to find that the crazy adventure of the past day and night had itself been some sort of virtual reality game, and that at any moment she would find herself back at Poker Bute Hall, getting into trouble again. *Was that possible?* she wondered. Could one go from one virtual reality game into another, and then another, like those Russian dolls that stacked inside each other? The thought of it made her head hurt, the way it did any time she contemplated the universe, or infinity.

The house was scarcely less fantastic than Fashionworld. The interior was like a series of bubbles, not a straight line anywhere. Some were small and windowless, cosy and cocoon-like; others were vast open spaces, their huge curved windows looking out onto the lush green gardens beyond.

'Your house is yoo-mungus!' exclaimed Elsie for about the fourth time, blinking in the daylight as they stepped from the cosy little gaming bubble into a huge living room.

Nolita smiled. 'Glad you like it! You guys didn't really get a chance to take anything in last night, did you?'

'I don't even remember coming here at *all*,' said Elsie. 'It was like waiting for Father Christmas – I was dying to stay awake for it, but I couldn't!' She had thought Nolita's office had been the most amazing place she had ever seen; this was even more fabulous.

Rorie, on the other hand, had made sure she had her wits about her when they'd arrived. Cammy, Nolita's maid, had offered to take her backpack for her, but Rorie had refused. For all she knew, Cammy would interfere with the rather odd assortment of second-hand clothing contained in it; she might even dispose of them in favour of better, newer things. That couldn't happen! Rorie refused to let them out of her sight, even for an instant. 'No!' she'd snapped – a little too fiercely – and yanked the backpack out of Cammy's reach.

Nolita had stared at her, wide-eyed. 'She only wants to put your things away, Rorie.'

'It's OK,' Rorie had insisted, clutching it protectively like a toddler with a favourite toy. '*I'll* do it. Really.'

Nolita and Cammy had looked at each other. Cammy shrugged, and spread her hands. 'OK!'

And that was that. For now, Rorie's Big Secret was safe. Only she and Elsie knew, and she had made a point of impressing on Elsie that she wasn't to tell anybody – not even Nolita.

As they emerged from the living room into the entrance lobby, various people were coming and going, all looking very busy, either carrying equipment or talking on their Shels[1].

'What's going on?' asked Rorie.

'Huh? Oh, this?' said Nolita casually. 'This is just everyday stuff, hon. Always lots going on.' She stopped briefly to talk to this one and that one as she went along, introducing Rorie and Elsie. Everyone greeted them enthusiastically.

---

1. Stands for See Hear Everything Live. Like a mini-computer, it's a phone, document file, camera, music and video player all in one.

Elsie was quite delirious with excitement over it all. 'I feel like a movie star or something!' she exclaimed.

'Hey, you're with me. Of course you're a star!' quipped Nolita, who was famed not only for her influence in the world of fashion, but for having 'discovered' a great number of celebrities. 'And stars need a little space to shine, don't you think? Let's go outside.'

From the garden, the house looked like a giant, semi-melted dollop of ice cream. Perched among the trees and hedges were a number of large, colourful sculptures, glistening in the early spring sunlight. They were bold, blobby shapes, vaguely humanoid, all female-looking, all flamboyantly embellished. The overall effect was one of a pageant of bizarre beauties.

'I call them my muses,' said Nolita.

'Wow,' said Rorie. 'They're weird, but...I like them!' Wandering among these strange creatures, she had the feeling that no one could ever be miserable in such a place.

The electronic hum of the gates opening prompted them to look up. 'Looks like we got a visit from the police,' said Nolita.

'Inspector Dixon!' cried Elsie, jumping up and down. 'Hey, maybe they found Mum and Dad!'

Chapter 2
Retail Therapy

'Just thought I'd stop by and see how you're doing,' said Inspector Dixon cheerfully, as he followed Nolita and the girls through the lobby.

Rorie felt despondent. 'So you don't have –'

Inspector Dixon didn't seem to hear her; he had stopped dead in his tracks, and was staring at a woman among the throng. 'Is that...? No, it can't be!'

'Iva Pasquale?' said Nolita casually. 'Yes, that's her.'

Inspector Dixon's face flushed red. 'I'm her biggest fan! I've seen all her movies.'

'I can introduce you later, if you like,' suggested Nolita.

'Really? Oh, that'd be great, Miss Newbuck, I...' Dixon trailed off, as his gaze settled on Rorie, who was staring forlornly at the floor. For a few blissful moments in Fashionworld, Rorie had actually forgotten all about Mum and Dad. Now, this glittering, larger-than-life world deflated like candyfloss dissolving in her mouth, as once again she felt the full force of her loss.

'Oh, Rorie, I'm sorry!' said Inspector Dixon. 'Stupid me! Here I am, banging on about Iva Pasquale...I should have realised that my coming here like this might get your hopes up.'

Rorie shrugged. 'It's OK.'

'Well, I just wanted to see that everything was all right, especially after all you've been through,' said Dixon, as Nolita led them to a more private place where they could sit. 'You'll be pleased to know your uncle has been suspended.'

'Suspended?'

'Yes. He's not allowed to run Poker Bute Hall. And, of course, the chances are he'll do a stretch in prison.' When Rorie and Elsie had run away and found refuge with Nolita, Uncle Harris had tried to abduct them. He had also tried to get their ailing great-grandmother to change her will in his favour, leaving him her millions.

'Has the school closed down?' asked Nolita, as they all sat down.

'No,' said Dixon, to groans of disappointment from

24

Rorie and Elsie. 'His wife's running it.'

Rorie pictured the bulldog Aunt Irmine, barking out orders at terrified Poker Bute Hall girls. And those scarily perfect Perfects, like the ice-queen Nikki Deeds, helping to enforce her strict regime. Then she thought of Moll, poor Moll...

'Well, it should be closed down!' declared Elsie indignantly. 'Can't *you* fix that?' she asked Dixon.

The policeman sighed. 'I'm afraid not. We've taken the criminal away from the place; there's nothing criminal about the school itself.'

'But –' Rorie began, then faltered.

'Yes, Rorie?'

'I...well, it's just that...' Rorie trailed off. What could she say? Everything she thought of came down to Uncle Harris. Aunt Irmine hadn't done anything illegal – not as far as she knew. But there had seemed to be something very sinister about Poker Bute Hall; something that went beyond just the loathsomeness of her uncle and aunt. The trouble was, she couldn't pinpoint what it was. It was no more than a hunch. In any case, there were other, more pressing issues to consider. 'Oh, Inspector!' she sighed. 'When are we going to hear something about Mum and Dad? It's been so long!'

'Believe it or not, these *are* still early days,' said Dixon gently. 'It's not even three weeks yet...I know!' He threw his hands up. 'It feels much longer to you...I understand that, really I do. But there is plenty more we can do.' He scratched his head. 'I won't pretend it isn't perplexing – quite mysterious, how they disappeared. We have that picture of the car from the speed camera – and then, pffft! Nothing. But we continue to search.'

'Where are you looking now?' asked Rorie.

'We've moved on to the area surrounding the collapsed tunnel – now that we've eliminated the possibility that your parents were...you know...'

Crushed by it, thought Rorie, reliving again that last morning before Mum and Dad had left for their big presentation to Rexco. It was, at least, something she could cling to – the knowledge that Mum and Dad had escaped that particular fate. It was still possible, however, that they had survived some sort of accident; there had initially been some speculation that they had both sustained head injuries and were suffering severe memory loss – amnesia. Elsie in particular found this idea comforting. 'They're gonna come home when they've got over their amneezer,' she always told people. Yet secretly Rorie couldn't believe this was

26

possible after all this time. She was sure Dixon thought the same thing, but was afraid to ask him. She didn't want to hear it out loud.

'They've been talking to us in our dreams,' Elsie remarked forlornly. 'Rorie had one last night, didn't you, Rorie?'

'Yes.' Rorie's dreams of Mum and Dad often featured a butterfly. It had come to symbolise for her not just the inspiration which made them able to invent things, but something bigger than that – the inspiration it would take to solve the terrible mystery of what had happened to them. It was a big, beautiful butterfly, and as was the way with such things, it was always wafting teasingly in and out of sight.

'An' I dreamt I had a magic dress, just like the one they invented,' said Elsie, recalling Mum and Dad's extraordinary demonstration of clothing that could be manipulated into any number of shapes, colours and patterns, all at the press of a button, or even with a verbal command. It really had been like magic. Then suddenly she stood up. 'Oh no!'

Dixon looked startled. 'What is it, Elsie?'

'The inventions! Maybe somebody kidnapped Mum'n'Dad, 'cause they wanted the magic dress, an' the superbootshoes, and—'

'Elsie,' said Inspector Dixon gently.

'Just like Uncle Harris tried to kidnap us...maybe he's in with some people that—'

'Elsie, *please*,' said Dixon more firmly. 'Sit down.'

'Yes, hon, calm down,' agreed Nolita, taking Elsie's hand.

Elsie sat, but she was shaking. Rorie put her arm around her. She had had similar thoughts herself, staring into the dark at three o'clock in the morning, but had rejected them in the cold light of day.

'We've thought of the kidnap scenario,' explained Dixon gently. 'Of course we have. I just haven't said anything because I didn't want to plant the idea in your heads – and in any case, it's not very likely.'

'It isn't?'

Dixon smiled and shook his head. 'Not really.'

'But...'

'Inspector Dixon has a point, Else,' said Rorie. 'Nobody else knew about those inventions besides Rexco – not even Uncle Harris.'

'Yes, we checked that out,' said Inspector Dixon. 'But we consider every possibility, and continue to explore all avenues.'

'What about Rexco?' asked Elsie. 'Maybe it was them.'

'I'm afraid that wouldn't make any sense, Elsie,' said Dixon. 'They're extremely concerned as to what might have happened to your parents and their inventions – which they were almost certainly going to buy.'

'Well, I –'

Nolita patted Elsie's hand. 'Elsie, I think you've gotten ideas from your experience with your uncle, hon.'

'Not to mention Nikki Deeds,' added Rorie, shuddering as she recalled the way that ice-queen of a Perfect had acted as Uncle Harris's accomplice.

'Yes, really Elsie. You're letting your imagination run away with you!' said Nolita. She spotted a bag Dixon was holding. 'Inspector, is that something you brought for the girls?'

'Oh! Yes,' said Dixon, glancing down. 'Miss Newbuck, I'm, er, not really supposed to do this, but…well, I brought some things for the girls from their home. Seems their uncle didn't let them take anything much to Poker Bute Hall.'

All thoughts of kidnaps instantly flew out of Elsie's mind. 'Oh, thank you!'

The girls delved into the bag. Inside was Rorie's collection of model chameleons, some of Elsie's soft toys and dolls, and a favourite scrunchy for tying her hair back that Mum had made. Elsie put it on straight away.

'And there's...this,' added Inspector Dixon, handing over a small envelope. 'It's a memory card with your home movies, photos...I thought it would be important for you to keep that stuff with you. I know if it was me, that's what I'd want.'

Rorie gasped, and reached for the envelope. 'Thank you!'

Dixon was hesitant. 'But...'

'What?'

'Just be careful, that's all,' he warned. 'I mean, I wanted you to have this, just so that you know it's safe. And perhaps Nolita can print off some pictures. But I'm not sure it's a good idea to watch the films. Happy memories can have a habit of making the present seem...well, you know what I mean.'

'I understand, Inspector,' said Nolita. 'I'll keep an eye on things.'

Dixon stood up to leave, and they followed him. 'Oh, and one more thing: I'm sending you my direct line number...there,' he said, hitting some buttons on his Shel. 'You might want to set it up for emergency alert – not that I think you'll need it; it's just for peace of mind, and all that. Best way to reach me quickly. Well, goodbye.'

'Nolita?' said Elsie, fiddling with the scrunchy in her hair as they stood on the steps, watching Inspector Dixon's car disappear through the gates. 'Yesterday you said *you* could help us find our parents. When you gonna start?'

'Elsie!' exclaimed Rorie. 'I don't think it's as simple as that.'

Nolita laughed. 'It's OK. Sure I'll help, any way I can. I'll keep those guys on their toes, I promise you.'

'But can't you find them yourself?' asked Elsie, bemused. 'I mean, you're famous!'

Rorie sighed. 'Elsie, being famous doesn't mean you're like, a *god* or something!'

'It doesn't?'

Under different circumstances, the look on Elsie's face at that moment would have made Rorie giggle…but she was in no mood to laugh. She realised she'd been wrong about Nolita's garden – she was miserable now, and not even the crazy sculptures could cheer her up. If anything, their joyful and proud expressions seemed to mock her.

'No, Elsie,' she said, her voice trembling. 'It doesn't.'

Nolita put an arm around each of them. 'Oh hey, *guys*,' she said softly.

'Could we watch some of those home movies?' asked Rorie.

'Maybe later,' said Nolita. 'Hey, you wanna know what I do when I'm down in the dumps?' she added brightly.

Rorie did her best to swallow the lump that was rising in her throat. 'What?'

Nolita beamed, and the diamond in her tooth twinkled. 'I get a new outfit. Retail therapy, never fails! So, whaddaya say we do the same for you?'

Elsie brightened a little. 'Get a new outfit?'

'Or five! Or six! Or twelve!' said Nolita. 'You need a whole new wardrobe, hon. How about it, Rorie?'

'Um, well, I guess we do need some stuff...'

'A whole new wardrobe!' gasped Elsie. 'Where'll we go?'

Nolita waved this off. 'Oh, Nolita doesn't go to the shops; the shops come to Nolita. Come on, I'll show you...Tinky?' She called her stylist on her Shel. 'Hold the fort while I kit the girls out, will you? Thanks, bye!'

Chapter 3
The Necklace

'Oh, Rorie!' cried Elsie, as she leapt onto her sister's bed in her brand-new peony-print pyjamas. 'Isn't Nolita just the most wonderful person in the whole wide world?'

'All right, I wouldn't go *that* far,' said Rorie, slipping between the soft, silky sheets.

'Whaddaya mean?' replied Elsie indignantly. 'She's fantastic! This was the best idea of mine, wasn't it?'

Rorie gave her a sideways look. True, it *had* been Elsie's idea to worm their way into Nolita's life, once the opportunity presented itself. But she really couldn't take the credit for everything that had happened since. 'OK, not a *completely* lousy idea as it turns out,' she admitted grudgingly, 'but you know what? Every time I think I've figured out how your mind works, you come out with another completely dumb thing.'

'Like what?'

'Like, "Oh, you're famous, you can fix anything!" I mean, really! You think you knew all along that Nolita would take us under her wing, don't you? Well, you're wrong!'

'Uh! I am so *not* wrong!' gasped Elsie. 'It happened, didn't it?'

'Yes, but...' Rorie trailed off. What was she trying to prove? Elsie's silly boasting might be irritating, but what did it really matter? 'Oh, never mind,' she said at last. 'All I meant was, you shouldn't think Nolita's like, your fairy godmother or something.'

Elsie wasn't listening; for the umpteenth time, she was trying on the new shoes Nolita had bought her. A few things had been sent round from some of Nolita's favourite stores, while plenty of other clothes had been ordered through Fashionworld, where Rorie and Elsie had been able to try out virtual outfits.

'I *love* these,' said Elsie, parading around in the red patent pumps. 'I feel like...Cinderella at the ball!'

Rorie toyed with the sleeve of her own crisp new pyjamas. 'Nolita *has* been amazingly kind and generous,' she admitted. 'It's just...I don't know, I can't believe it all, somehow. I guess I just don't really *know* her yet.'

'But you do know her. She's—'

'Famous, *right*,' interrupted Rorie, unable to stop the sarcasm from creeping into her voice. 'Else, that isn't the same as *really* knowing someone. You don't know her either. You think you do, but you don't.'

'Do *too*.'

'Do *not*.'

'I do so,' retorted Elsie, slumping onto Rorie's bed and kicking off her shoes petulantly. 'And it's very boring of you not to be excited. Borie Rorie, borie Rorie—'

Rorie shoved her legs sharply down the bedclothes, dislodging Elsie so that she toppled to the floor. 'Ha ha!'

Elsie picked up a pillow and whirled it at Rorie's head. Rorie ducked, and Elsie ended up falling sideways with the force of the throw. Rorie laughed again.

'I'm gonna get you!' cried Elsie, lunging at her sister.

Rorie caught her arm and held it firm. 'Hey! Aren't you forgetting something?' she said, serious now. 'You wouldn't even have had the *chance* to get us here if it weren't for me! *I* got us out of Poker Bute Hall, so just you be grateful.' She released Elsie's arm.

'And anyway...why did Nolita have to change the subject like that, when we asked about finding Mum and Dad?'

Elsie shrugged, adjusting a bow on her pyjama top that had come undone. 'We needed stuff.'

'Oh, *right*,' said Rorie sarcastically.

Elsie went to her own bed and climbed in. '*I* think she's brilliant, anyway,' she said, her voice muffled in her pillow.

Rorie stared at the ceiling in silence. Part of her wished she too could be swept along by it all the way Elsie was. She was certainly relieved to be away from Uncle Harris and Poker Bute Hall. But from the moment they had escaped, she had felt as if she were caught up in a whirlwind; she just wanted things to be quiet for a while, so she could have room to think. Nolita's world was so different from anything she'd ever experienced. She could only suppose the rules were different if you were rich and famous, and taking in waifs and strays was just one more fun thing you could do that didn't cost too much, so why not? And it had happened so easily; as Nolita had said, she was a very powerful woman.

But how can she be so sure she wants us? Rorie wondered. After all, it worked both ways – Nolita

didn't know what she was getting into either. Unless...
Rorie had another thought: *Perhaps Nolita was secretly convinced their parents would soon return!* Or perhaps Inspector Dixon believed that – or both of them! But they weren't letting on, just in case. So everyone was just looking for a suitable arrangement until then, and *that* was why it wasn't a big deal...and why neither of them seemed to take the kidnap theory seriously. Having had the thought, Rorie savoured it for a moment, before mentally putting it away in a box and burying it. It really wouldn't do to hope such a thing.

But there were things Nolita didn't know. In particular, there was Rorie's Big Secret, about how she sometimes...*changed*. Nolita must never know about *that*. So far, Elsie hadn't mentioned it; but she was such a bigmouth, she might let it slip at any time. Rorie would have to convince her somehow that she must never say anything.

'Elsie?' she called softly. But Elsie was already fast asleep. *First thing in the morning*, Rorie told herself.

'You're not getting me into that!' exclaimed Rorie, as she fingered the tortuous pleats of the preposterously silly party dress she was supposed to wear for her first fashion shoot as Nolita's latest Young Teen Model.

'Oh yes we are,' said Tinky, thrusting the dress forward. 'Trust me, you'll look *amazing* in it. Come on, I ain't asking you to wear it out with yer mates!'

'Oh, all right,' said Rorie, and took the dress away to the cocoon-shaped dressing room. The dusky-pink dress made an expensive rustle as she pulled it on; it certainly *felt* nice. Rorie stepped into the matching pair of shoes, then looked in the mirror. She was quite startled by the transformation. She hadn't got used to the twisted-up hairstyle yet, or the make-up – she barely recognised herself.

'Oh boy, you look terrific!' exclaimed Tinky, as Rorie emerged from the cocoon. 'Quite a transformation, eh? Are you pleased?'

Rorie looked at herself in the mirror and twirled. 'It's…like it's not really me!'

'But it *is* you,' said Tinky.

No it isn't, Rorie felt like saying. *It's a fantasy version of me; it's not real.* 'Well, all right then,' she said aloud. 'It's Aurora.' Yes, 'Aurora' – the name 'Rorie' was short for – suited the person in the dress. She was like the dawn of a new day: fresh and delicate, rosy-hued, fleeting. A real thing after all, maybe, but not one that lasted. Not solid, permanent flesh and blood like Rorie Silk.

'Oh, but *Rorie* is a much better name for you,' declared Tinky. 'Don't you think, Mo?' she asked the photographer.

'Yeah, it's more sporty, the kids'll like it.'

Rorie disliked the way this reduced her own identity to something like an advertising slogan, but she let it pass. Right now she was rather enjoying being Aurora.

'A necklace,' said Tinky. 'Needs a necklace. Let's have a look.' She opened up a large jewellery box, which spread itself out into tiers of smaller boxes as she pushed back the lid. After rejecting a few possibilities, she held up a pretty gold-and-black-pearl creation. 'Ooh, now *this* would look lovely! Go on, try it on,' she suggested, handing it to Rorie.

'That's nice,' said Mo. 'Unusual. Where'd you get it?'

'It was my gran's, actually,' said Tinky.

Her gran's? thought Rorie, instinctively letting go. *Ker-splat!* went the necklace, as it fell to the floor. *No!* she thought. *My Big Secret will be out!* 'I'm sorry!' she squeaked. *Now what?* she wondered. She couldn't wear the necklace; she mustn't! Not if it had belonged to someone else...

The necklace was right by Rorie's feet, and Tinky clearly expected her to pick it up – but Rorie just stood there, frozen. Eventually Tinky picked it up herself and inspected it. 'All right, well, it's still in one piece. Here.' She held it out for Rorie to take.

'I – I can't,' said Rorie.

'What do you mean, you can't?'

What do I say? thought Rorie, her mind all aflutter. *'I'll turn into your gran'*? There she was, thinking she had everything under control because she'd remembered that morning to have a word with Elsie. She'd told her that Nolita must never know that Rorie changed like a chameleon whenever she put on someone else's clothes; if she found out, they'd be without a home again, since Nolita was bound to find it creepy and weird, just as the girls at Poker Bute Hall had done. And now this had to happen. 'I'm...allergic – *ahem* – to, um, pearls,' Rorie lied, then immediately regretted it. Suppose she were asked to wear another previously owned item, something other than pearls – what then?

'Really?' said Tinky. 'Wow. I never heard of that. You ever heard of that, Mo?'

Mo shook his head. 'New one on me.'

'Well. Never mind, eh?' said Tinky, delving back

into the jewellery box. 'Shame. It would have set it off ever so nice...how about this one?'

Rorie eyeballed the sculpted silver necklace and tried to figure out whether this one was old or new; she couldn't tell. 'Oh, uh, that's nice. Um, where did that one come from, then?' she asked, hoping it sounded like a casual enquiry.

'Ah, some supplier or other,' said Tink vaguely. 'We get sent stuff on loan all the time. Go on, try it.'

Rorie hesitated. What did that mean? Was it new or not? But she sensed impatience now, and if she asked any more questions she would definitely come across as a bit of a weirdo. She would have to risk it. 'Thank you,' she said, taking it. She put it on and, to her relief, nothing happened. And Tinky was happy with it, so they went off for the shoot.

Rorie was nervous to start with, but Mo was very kind and understanding. Of course, he assumed she was just a bit shaky because she'd never done a fashion shoot before; he didn't know it was because she'd been so afraid of being found out. In one sense, she felt like a freak – she hadn't had a lot of time to get used to the bizarre after-effects of being struck by lightning two weeks earlier...

Flash! went the camera, and Rorie was instantly transported back to that stormy night when she had been trying to run away from Poker Bute Hall, clutching her pet chameleon.

Flash! Then oblivion. Then a quiet funeral for a beloved pet. Soon followed by the discovery that she now had only to put on someone else's clothes, and she 'became' them. Or rather, her identity merged with theirs, in a similar way to a chameleon changing colour to match its surroundings. Not something she would readily share with others any time soon.

But on the other hand, it made her feel powerful, and she would protect her collection of 'borrowed' clothes at all costs. Nikki Deeds's trainers. Aunt Irmine's jacket. Leesa Simms's school cravat. Moll's necklace. Each one gave her some special skill she didn't ordinarily have. All may be well for now, but after everything she'd been through, who could say what was around the corner? She may find herself in need of them.

Flash! 'Lovely!' pronounced Mo. 'Well done, Rorie. I swear, it's like you're a different person in that dress!'

Chapter 4
Fabulosity

'It's out with those ghastly Nigerian-Elizabethan mini-crins!' announced Nolita. 'Now, take a look at India Hutton, stepping out in London last night; she has ditched that fussy, over-embellished look in favour of this lovely silver geometric design. I call it the Retro-Future look, and I predict this will be a hot new trend, so snap it up if you can!'

This was the moment that dictated what women everywhere would be wearing for the next seven days. Up and down the country, mini-crins were being thrown out; *everybody* wanted to be India Hutton that week, and nobody would be seen dead in last week's look. This was the ritual at ten o'clock every Saturday morning, as Nolita's blog went live – the start of a frantic race to get up-to-the-minute, to fall into line with what the Queen of Fashion dictated.

As they half watched Nolita's blog, Rorie and Elsie were trying on some of their new outfits in their luxurious new bedroom. 'Just think,' said Elsie, as she slipped into a pair of silver trousers, 'we're the bestest, most fashnable kids of *anyone* right now!'

'Mmm,' murmured Rorie distractedly. 'I'm hungry. Let's get some breakf—' She was interrupted by a knock at the door. 'Come in?'

'Hi, girls, how ya doin'?' said Tink, entering the room. 'Well, just look at you! Watchin' the blog, are ya? She's good, in't she?'

'I watch it *every* week,' declared Elsie solemnly.

'It's true,' said Rorie. 'Elsie's always been a fan.'

'How 'bout you?' asked Tink.

'Well…to be honest, I'm more of a slants person,' said Rorie.

'Not any more, you ain't!' joked Tinky, nudging her. 'Here, Nolita told me to give you these,' she added, handing them each a sheet of paper. 'Your schedules. Nolita decided you should be home-schooled. Good idea, eh?'

Rorie realised that with all the drama of the last couple of days, they had never even asked what was going to happen about school. There had been so much else to take in. She studied the schedule. 'Oh, look Elsie – when I'm doing my modelling sessions, you get to do "Wardrobe Studies"...'

'Dress-up, in other words,' said Tinky.

'...and Astrology...'

'Studying "the stars".'

'Oh, and look – we both get to do something called "Movie-ology" – and Art & Design!'

'Oh, wow!' gasped Elsie, beside herself with glee. Nothing even remotely creative had been allowed at Poker Bute Hall, let alone anything as enjoyable as 'Movie-ology' sounded. She peered over Rorie's shoulder, slipping her scrunchy off her wrist and tying her hair back. 'Games...music... What's "bussy ness"?'

'*Business* Studies,' corrected Rorie.

'That's when you spend time in the office,' explained Tinky. 'You'll learn a lot.'

'Hang on – what's "Fabulosity"?' asked Rorie.

'Oh, Chinchilla, your tutor, can explain far better than I can,' said Tinky. 'Make sure you check the location for each lesson; that one takes place in the summerhouse. And...' she glanced at her watch. 'You've just got time for a quick breakfast before you head down there. Bye-ee!'

*

'It's just what you think it is, darling,' said Chinchilla. 'Fabulosity is a most important lesson in life – the art of being fabulous! I work with all Nolita's new discoveries.'

'Oh,' said Rorie, still not sure if this was a joke of some sort. 'Is it a real word?'

'It is now!' said Chinchilla. 'Ha ha ha!' She tossed her head, with its mass of tumbling black curls. A flowing turquoise dress hung loosely from her glossy brown shoulders, and assorted ropes of beads and silky scarves were draped around her neck. Rorie found herself laughing along with her. *If anyone could teach fabulosity*, she thought, *here was the person.*

'Anyhow, darlings, let's get started!' said Chinchilla. She brought them over to a large mirror. 'Now, what you must know is that you are already fabulous – you just may not know it yet! Or you may *slightly* know it, but sixty or seventy per cent of the time you have your doubts. Am I right?'

'Uh, yeah,' agreed Rorie.

Elsie didn't answer, but Rorie knew that for all her apparent self-confidence, Elsie was convinced she was the ugliest child to walk the planet. Sometimes Rorie would feel embarrassed to notice that Elsie was gazing

46

at her wistfully, not understanding why she hadn't inherited that thick, glossy hair, almond eyes and full red lips.

'So say it to yourselves now,' urged Chinchilla. '"I am fabulous!" Go on! "I am fabulous!"'

Rorie mumbled the words, not looking herself in the eye.

Elsie was silent, frowning.

'What's the matter, Elsie?' asked Chinchilla.

'I need the dress-up,' said Elsie. 'I can only say that when I'm in dress-up.'

'Ah! Lesson number one: this is not about the clothes. And it's not about beauty, either. It's about *you*.'

'So I have to pretend?'

'To start with, yes,' beamed Chinchilla. 'Eventually, it will become fact.'

'You mean, just by saying it, we'll *become* fabulous?' asked Rorie.

'Yes!'

'Like magic?' suggested Elsie.

'Exactly. Now, try again: I – am – fabulous!'

Eventually, Rorie stopped worrying about how silly it all was, and from that point on she actually started to enjoy herself. Chinchilla was an exotic creature, whose world had clearly never involved bus journeys or washing-up or maths homework. She wore summer clothes all year round, and told them, 'Wear things that put a smile on your face!' That was a key part of Chinchilla's Philosophy of Life. She had probably never worried about anything more pressing than a bad-hair day, and Rorie found there was something quite wonderful about that. It gave her a lift, rather in the same way as the company of babies or animals did. With Chinchilla, everything really *did* seem fabulous.

And so the day's lessons whizzed by; a greater contrast to the dreary Poker Bute Hall could not have been dreamt up. For Art and Design, Tink had brought them over to Armando's Atelier. Armando, with his long white hair, sweeping black sideburns and shirt with oversized collar and cuffs, was just as flamboyant as Chinchilla. In fact, Rorie soon realised there wasn't a single person associated with Nolita who wasn't.

'Have you noticed,' she asked Elsie as they were getting ready for bed, 'how much Armando's place and the summerhouse are like this house? They're all great big bubbles.'

'I think bubbles are *lovely*,' sighed Elsie, as she went

over to the mirror. 'I can't think of anything nicer to live in!' She addressed her reflection. 'I am fabliuss.'

'*Fabulous*,' corrected Rorie.

'I. Yam. Fab-yoo-luss,' practised Elsie. 'And Mum and Dad are fine. And they're coming home soon. Yes! They're coming home soo-oo-oon!'

'Elsie, what are you on about?'

'If you say it enough, that makes it true,' declared Elsie confidently. 'Chinchilla *said*.'

Rorie sighed. 'Right. Chinchilla said. Oh, Else, if only it were that simple!'

'What's that, hon?' asked Nolita, who had just entered the room.

'Oh, it's just that Elsie's got it into her head that the mirror can make her wishes come true,' said Rorie.

'Well, Elsie, be careful what you wish for!' joked Nolita, apparently not having heard her pleas for her parents' safe return. 'Night-night, honeybunches.'

'Nolita?' said Rorie. '*Can* you help us find Mum and Dad? Really?'

'Well, now, I think your Inspector Dixon seems to know his stuff, don't you?' Nolita said brightly.

'Yes but—'

Nolita's Shel rang. 'Oh, hon, so sorry, gotta take

this call...big hug! Mwah, mwah!' She air-kissed them both. 'Hi...yeah...' She waved to the girls flamboyantly as she left the room.

Rorie sat on the bed and looked across at Elsie. Her face was filled with sadness.

Chapter 5
Ragged Trousers

'Velcome to my laboratory!' said the wild-eyed man in a white coat and a ridiculous bird's-nest wig. The wobbly camera followed him into the basement room, and stifled giggles could be heard.

'Oh, wow – it feels like a lifetime since I last saw this!' said Rorie, as she sat watching the film in the darkened room with Elsie. The 'Mad Professor' was really their father, Arran Silk, looning around for Rorie's camera in his real-life laboratory.

It was Saturday evening, and Nolita was out. 'Busy night tonight, I'm afraid,' she'd explained, consulting her Shel. 'I have four...five...six parties to go to.' She flipped it shut. 'I'll only spend fifteen minutes at each of them, but it's essential that I go. Anyway, you two look bushed – get some rest!' she'd added, ruffling Elsie's hair affectionately. And then she was gone.

'Now, in zis experiment,' said the Mad Professor, flicking his hair out of his eyes, 'I shall attempt to make a mountain out of a molehill. For zis I shall need ze help of my lovely assistant, Laura...'

The camera swerved over, and a woman in a frumpy fringed hairdo and heavy-framed spectacles – Mum – came into view, carrying a tray with a mound of some sort of greyish matter. This, the girls knew, was in fact a pile of the fibres used in their thinfat jackets, which swelled or shrank according to the temperature. It was old technology, but since the girls seldom got demonstrations of Dad's new inventions, he and Mum often used to amuse them with shows like this one.

Laura gurned idiotically at the camera as she put the tray down in front of the professor.

'Sank you, Laura,' said the professor. 'You vill make somevone a lovely vife some day!' He buried his hand in the 'molehill'. 'Ah! Complete viz a gen-u-ine mole, I see!' he remarked, pulling out a little toy mouse. 'Vell, ve can leave him be, he vill be unaffected by ze trransformation. OK, now Laura, ze drry ice, please!'

Mum donned a pair of gloves and brought over a gas canister, which she then sprayed onto the mound.

A great cloud of dry ice formed, and when it cleared, the mound was ten times its original size. 'Excellent!' said the Mad Professor, emerging from behind it. 'Vell, as you can see, ve haff some success – not quite mountain-sized, maybe, but – aargh! Vot iss zat monster?'

The camera whizzed across to Laura, who was now wrestling with an alarmingly large black furry thing. 'It's the mole, professor. Aargh!'

'Oh my goodness, zis is a wholly unexpected rresult!' exclaimed the professor, hair going wild. 'How marvellous; just sink of ze possibilities!'

Meanwhile, Laura was screaming as she made a very convincing act of being under attack from the 'mutant mole'.

The professor was oblivious. 'Going horseback riding on ze family dog! Scaring avay ze foxes viz a giant chicken...vot fun!'

'Aargh, help!' cried Laura, then the words 'The End' filled the screen, followed by Rorie's list of credits.

It used to make them laugh. Now, Elsie and Rorie stared blankly at the screen. 'Well, erm, what next then?' said Rorie, as she flipped the controls on the remote. Then she made eye contact with Elsie, and the two of them dissolved into tears.

'Oohh, I miss them so much!' wailed Elsie.

'So do I,' muttered Rorie, her voice thick with tears.

'What on earth is going on here?' came a voice from behind them.

The girls looked up and saw Nolita, silhouetted in the doorway. 'We were...' attempted Rorie, before breaking down in tears once again.

Nolita trotted swiftly towards them down the aisle of the small private auditorium. Today her hair was woven with blue strands, and she wore an electric-blue dress that swished gently as she moved. 'Oh hey, you poor babies!' She looked at the screen, which now displayed a group of stills from an assortment of Rorie's home movies, with the titles alongside them. A cartoon chameleon hovered over one of them, with a speech bubble saying 'Play'.

'You were watching your old home movies, weren't you?'

'Yes.'

Nolita gently took the remote out of Rorie's lap and switched the system off, then turned up the house lights. 'And look what it's done; it's only gotten you all upset.'

Elsie sniffed loudly. 'I still don't see why you can't

get Mum and Dad back for us,' she said softly.

Nolita was silent for a moment, then sat down next to them. Her eyes were an intense blue today, to match her outfit. 'OK, listen. I'm gonna tell you a story – and it's a true story. When I was seven years old – same age as you, Elsie – my dad went down to the convenience store to buy some Spray-Fix; you know, the stuff that mends tears in fabric? We needed it for some pants of mine – sorry, *trousers*; the knees were worn through. He didn't want me playing with the kids in the street looking like that. I waited indoors, while the other kids played. Three times my friends came to the door to ask for me, but my mom told them I was busy doing homework. The truth was, I had only one other pair of pants, but they were my good ones and I wasn't allowed to play on the street in them.'

Rorie tried to picture the little Nolita in her ripped pair of trousers – a small ragamuffin. It was almost impossible to imagine.

'Eventually, my mom and I went down to the convenience store, ripped pants and all,' Nolita went on. 'But no one knew where Dad was. Mom figured maybe he'd gone to the dollar store on Broadway, so we tried there – nothing. And we searched on and on, until it grew dark.

'Dad didn't come back that night, or ever again. I stopped playing with the kids on the block. I told them I had to wait for my dad to fix my pants. Even when my mom fixed them, I still wouldn't play, because it wasn't the same; they were supposed to be fixed by Dad. For a whole year I didn't play. Finally, over breakfast one morning, my mom snapped. "He's not coming back," she announced. We sold everything, and moved in with my grandparents. It wasn't great, but I made new friends on the block, started a new school, and…everything was OK. Not *great*, but…life went on.'

There was a pause.

'You don't think our parents are coming back, do you?' said Rorie morosely, staring at the floor.

'What I'm saying is, it's out of your hands,' said Nolita. 'I'm publicising it all I can…but the best thing you can do is just get on with your lives and not expect them to come back. Don't be like I was, wishing my life away, waiting for my dad to walk in with a can of Spray-Fix.'

Suddenly, Rorie saw Nolita in a whole new light. It had never occurred to her that she might once have been poor, let alone have lost a parent in such a way. To have lost so much, even when one had so little in the first place – no wonder Nolita liked so much to acquire things. She even wondered if collecting people might be seen as a way of making up for that loss. Especially ones who turn up the way they had: in ragged trousers.

Chapter 6
Power Boots

'Rorie! Over here, Rorie!' yelled the crowd. 'Nolita! Rorie!' they went, over and over again.

'OK, heads down and...dash!' instructed Nolita, and together with Rorie and Elsie, she splashed through the rain to the car, armed against the throng of reporters with a giant umbrella. It was Sunday afternoon, and they were on their way to the country house of one of Nolita's discoveries.

'Oh boy,' sighed Nolita, as the driver moved slowly off, honking loudly to part the crowd. 'Paparazzi! My worst occupational hazard.'

Rorie felt her heart pounding as she sat, head on her knees, rainwater dripping from her nose. She was not prepared for this.

'Don't worry,' said Nolita, patting her on the back. 'It's the novelty factor. They're curious about the two kids now living with Nolita Newbuck – especially since I did the piece about your parents. They'll soon lose interest in you, I promise – in about a week's time is my guess. I should know. It's why I have to keep inventing more stars for them to obsess over.'

Rorie thought about this. 'What happens to the old ones, then?'

But her voice was drowned out by the paparazzi pounding on the window, and she didn't get a reply.

Getting away on Monday morning was easier, as they were going to Nolita's office, and that meant taking Nolita's own private underground shuttle. Rorie and Elsie had travelled on it on their first night with Nolita, but had been too exhausted to appreciate it. This time they were only too glad to be hidden away from the paparazzi.

'Hey, starlet!' cried Artie, embracing Rorie as they emerged from the elevator into the lobby of Nolita's office.

'Don't call me that!' scolded Rorie with mock anger. She liked Artie a lot. Not only was he friendly and funny, but he was just as colourful as Nolita, with his metallic green and violet close-cropped hair.

'We are going to have such a fun day!' declared Artie.

'It's our Business Studies lesson,' said Rorie, sceptical. It didn't sound much fun.

'Piece o' cake,' said Artie, busying himself with sorting some items on his desk. 'All you do? Is just tag along with me all day! And I explain everything as we go along. How does that sound, eh, little Miss Elsie?'

Elsie was already over by the window, gazing out at all of London below. 'Cool!'

Later that day, some rails of clothes were delivered, and the girls accompanied Artie as he took them to the Collection.

'Wow!' gasped Elsie. 'This place is amazing!' The Collection was like an Aladdin's cave of fashion. Incredible outfits hung on racks and mannequins, surrounded by red walls and floor-to-ceiling mirrors.

'Yes, honey, but we have to lock up now,' said Artie. 'Work to do. Come along. No – don't touch that! That belongs to India Hutton!'

'It does? And these things?' asked Elsie, fingering another rail of clothes.

'Elsie!' scolded Rorie.

'Those are Nolita's,' said Artie. 'She often changes

in the daytime. You know, I'd love to be able to let you stay in here, Elsie, but I can't. Someone would have to stay with you, and no one's free. Come along.'

'OK,' said Elsie, despondently.

But the genie was out of the bottle; now that Elsie knew about the Collection, she was interested in nothing else and was beginning to make a pest of herself. Eventually Nolita called Cammy and asked her to come and take Elsie home.

'But now you're here, *you* can take me into the Collection, right?' Elsie asked Cammy when she arrived. '*Please?*'

'All right,' said Cammy. 'But not for too long, OK?'

A little later, Artie sent Rorie to the Collection, to retrieve the India Hutton clothes. It *was* rather thrilling; she could understand why Elsie had been so enthralled with the place.

'Hey, Rorie, over here!' came her sister's voice from somewhere among the finery.

'Not now, Else, I'm busy,' Rorie called back.

'Just for a *minute*. Come and look!'

'Oh all right. Where are you? Oh...*oh*.' Her voice dropped as she caught sight of the shimmering frock that Elsie was wearing, so big on her that the hem

61

grazed the floor. Rorie felt a sudden stab of indescribable sadness.

'Isn't it great?' said Elsie, giving a twirl. 'It's a—'

'A Changing Picture Dress. Yes, I know,' interrupted Rorie flatly, noticing the digitised fabric that the owner could upload images onto.

'What's the matter?' asked Elsie, deflated. 'Don't you like the picture?'

'No, it's not that,' said Rorie. In fact, the picture was ridiculous – an oversized photograph of cute puppies with big blue bows around their necks – but that wasn't what was troubling Rorie. 'Mum used to have one of those,' she explained.

'What, a puppy? Oh – you mean the dress.'

'I guess you wouldn't remember,' said Rorie. 'It was a few years ago. It broke. That one must be pretty old – I don't think they make them any more.'

Elsie was silent for a moment. The puppies disappeared, replaced by a large, staring cat. 'It's Nolita's favourite dress,' she said despondently. 'It's vintish.'

'You mean *vintage*,' corrected Rorie.

Then Artie appeared. 'Make sure you put everything back right, loves. Wardrobe assistant's off today. Ooh, you'd better be careful with that one,' he added, looking at the Changing Picture Dress, which now displayed a kitten in a wineglass. 'Did you get permission?'

'Sorry. We were just putting it away,' said Cammy, hurriedly de-powering the dress with the button on its shoulder. The kitten dissolved into blankness; Elsie gazed down at it despondently.

Artie winked at Elsie. 'It's OK, I won't tell.'

'Oh, Artie, sorry,' said Rorie, 'I was looking for those things and—'

'Oh, that's not why I'm here,' said Artie, making his way over to a double-doored cupboard. 'Her ladyship's ready to reboot.'

'To what?' asked Rorie.

Artie gave a mischievous chuckle as he opened up the cupboard. Inside was row upon row of boots. Platform boots, wedge-heeled boots, boots in suede, patent leather, metallic leather – boots of every conceivable colour. 'Nolita's collection of Power Boots!' said Artie. 'You ever notice that's what she always wears?'

Rorie thought. 'Well, yeah actually, now you come to mention it.'

'And...any second now...' Artie's Shel sprang to life, and Nolita appeared on its screen.

'Artie, where are you? I said I'm ready to reboot!'

'Just coming, Nolita. Mauve OK?' he asked, picking out a pair.

'Yup.' The screen went blank.

'I am naughty!' chuckled Artie. He nudged Rorie conspiratorially. 'I love her really,' he added, then headed back out to the office with the boots.

Rorie followed, and Elsie trotted behind, hastily doing up her slants and slipping into her shoes. 'Wait for me!'

'Shh!' said Artie, finger to lips. 'She needs quiet while she's with her reflexologist.'

The office was hushed, all lights dimmed. Nolita sat reclined in her seat, eyes closed; she didn't stir as Artie approached with the boots. A woman in a white coat was massaging her bare feet, and murmuring something that Rorie couldn't quite make out. She had a soothing voice, light as a gentle breeze.

Then the woman retreated, and light and sound flooded the room once more. Nolita sat up and blinked. 'Not too fast, Nolita,' warned the woman. 'Take your time.'

'OK, Misty,' said Nolita. Her eyes were unfocused, and for a moment she seemed to Rorie like a sleepwalking child, still unaware of all around her;

the effect was rather disturbing. Then suddenly she was herself again. 'Ahh, thank you, Misty,' she said, pulling on the mauve boots. 'That's better!'

Misty nodded, her pale, doll-like face without expression but for the slight curl at the corner of her tiny rosebud lips. 'Of course it is, Nolita. Much better.'

'Why'd you do that?' Elsie asked Nolita.

Nolita stuck her legs out and flexed her ankles. 'I reboot at least once a day,' she explained. 'It helps whenever I'm going stale, running out of ideas.'

Elsie looked confused. 'So you fink with your feet?'

'I think *on* my feet,' Nolita corrected.

'She's always on her toes, isn't that right, Nolita?' said Artie. 'Gets an idea and she *runs* with it.'

'OK, I'm ready,' said Nolita, pointing the remote at the screen. 'Got a little stuck there on the latest NBT.'

'NBT?' echoed Rorie.

'Next Big Thing,' said Nolita. 'Got Next Little Things happening all the time, but every now and then you gotta have a radical fashion concept – keeps the public interested. 'Cause what the stars wear today, the public wears tomorrow. Can't afford to get it wrong. I talk to designers every day – half the time *they* come to *me* for their NBT!'

'Do you *ever* stop working?' asked Elsie.

'Never!' laughed Nolita. 'Only when I'm sleeping. Work is play, and play is work – there's no difference. Now scram, honeybunches, I got thinkin' to do. Catch you later!'

As they shot through the shuttle tunnel on their way home, Elsie prattled away to Cammy about all the thrilling things she'd seen in the Collection. Rorie's mind wandered; she realised that this was the first time she'd ever seen Nolita sit still – and even that was just so she could recharge for yet more work. Even Dad didn't seem as obsessed with work as Nolita – and Dad was pretty fixated. *How much does she really get out of having us around?* Rorie wondered. It all made her feel ever so slightly like that favourite dress of Nolita's, stuck away in the Collection: admired on occasion, ignored the rest of the time. *Oh, stop it!* Rorie told herself. She really shouldn't fill her head with such negative thoughts. She should give Nolita a chance – it had only been four days, after all! She forced herself to think of Poker Bute Hall, which made things seem better, until thoughts of the Changing Picture Dress crept in and she remembered the one Mum had worn until it broke. 'Not made to last,' Mum had sighed. 'Just like everything else! One component goes, and *pfft!* that's it. Bye-bye, get a new one.'

'Not the way we work,' Dad had remarked.

'No,' agreed Mum. 'If something's worth having, it's worth having for ever...'

Could they have been kidnapped? Rorie asked herself. But try as she might, she just couldn't see how anyone else could have known about Mum and Dad's latest inventions...

Chapter 7
Secret Weapon

'Guess what,' said Elsie, breathless with excitement, when Rorie came home from a modelling session.

Rorie looked her up and down. Elsie was draped in a bizarre assortment of ill-fitting garments, while other clothes were strewn in tangled heaps about the bedroom floor. 'We've been burgled?' she asked sarcastically. It was Friday afternoon – she was exhausted and not at all in the mood for this. She had never thought modelling could be such hard work. But it felt good to know she was earning money, accumulating in a bank account somewhere; it made her feel very grown-up.

'No, silly!' said Elsie. 'I'm designering.'

'You mean *designing*. And I never saw someone who so *didn't* look as if they were designing something, Elsie.'

'Yes but Armando said I could start my own fashion label, and Nolita gave me some of her old clothes to cut up and make new stuff with, and it's gonna be called "Elsie's Favorit Froxx", whaddaya think?'

Rorie flopped onto the bed. 'Amazing.'

'I think it's gonna be *mega*-amazing,' declared Elsie, as she posed this way and that in front of the mirror, adjusting the drapery to her liking. 'I mean, I like doing that Fashionworld stuff, but it's more fun with the actual cloves.'

Rorie said nothing. Elsie paused, then picked up a shirt. 'Hey, Rorie?' she said, her voice lowering.

'Mmm? Oh...no,' said Rorie, spotting the mischievous gleam in Elsie's eye as she came towards her – she wanted a chameleon show. 'No, Elsie, I am *not* putting it on.'

'Oh go on, pleeeease?' wheedled Elsie.

Rorie waved her off. 'Go away, I'm tired.'

'But I really want to see what happens!' insisted Elsie.

'Look, I haven't any reason –'

'Yes, you have. Fun,' said Elsie. 'Do it for meee, Roreeee!' She pressed the shirt to Rorie's chest.

Rorie sighed loudly and rolled her eyes. Part of her

was curious to see what she looked like as Nolita…

'All right, if it'll make you shut up,' she said, taking the shirt. 'But just this once, OK? I'm not a circus act, you know. Plus, it's secret. Don't forget our agreement.'

'Yeah, I know,' said Elsie hurriedly. She jumped up and down impatiently. 'Come on then!'

Rorie took a deep breath and reached out for the shirt, but found herself trembling with nerves. She let it go and it fell to the ground.

'What's the matter?' asked Elsie.

Rorie was genuinely perplexed. 'I don't know… suddenly this feels like a weird thing to do to someone. Like spying on them, or something. I guess I never did it with clothes belonging to anyone I was this close to before. Seems…disrespectful, somehow.'

'Don't be silly,' said Elsie, picking up the shirt again. 'You're not spying. It's just for fun.'

'I suppose…' Rorie took the shirt and forced herself to put it on. She shut her eyes tight. 'OK. Tell me when I'm done.'

Now she realised that it wasn't just the sense of intrusion that troubled her, it was something more. The whole idea of transforming disturbed her, probably from her experiences of changing into some pretty hideous, evil people, like Aunt Irmine. But Nolita wasn't hideous or evil! Nor did she apparently have any major character flaw, like Pat Dry and her drink problem...

'You know, the other thing is, I don't like not being me, full stop,' she told Elsie, her eyes still tight shut. 'I mean, what if I got stuck like that? Ugh!' she shivered. 'Am I done yet?'

'Nope,' said Elsie. 'Hasn't even started.'

Rorie opened one eye. '*Nothing?*'

'Uh-uh.'

Rorie, her curiosity awakened now, opened the other eye and looked at herself in the mirror; she was completely unchanged.

'Oh! Well...that's weird. Huh.' She stared at her normal reflection, suddenly awash with disappointment. 'I guess I'm cured.'

'Oh, no!' gasped Elsie. 'You can't be!'

And, in spite of her reservations, Rorie found that she felt the same frustration. She had grown used to her chameleon quality; it was her special secret power, and the idea that it might have deserted her was sending her into a state of mild panic. 'No, this can't be right!' she said, undoing the shirt. She pulled on a pair of Nolita's trousers and waited. Nothing happened. 'No!' she cried. She tried a top and a dress and a jacket. Nothing.

Then something struck her. 'Hang on, how long has Nolita had these things, do you suppose?'

'I dunno,' said Elsie. 'But she only just had a big clear-out the other day.'

Rorie clicked her fingers. 'That's it! *Of course* I'm not changing – Nolita's probably only worn these things once or twice! She hasn't had them long enough for them to...I don't know, absorb all that Nolita-ness or whatever.'

'*Oh!*' said Elsie. 'So put on something she's had longer, then.'

'But that's my point: I don't think she ever hangs on to her things for any length of time!'

'Well, there's the Changing Picture Dress,' Elsie reminded her. 'She's had that for ages.'

'OK, but that's in the Collection at the office,' said Rorie, pulling on her bathrobe. 'Hey, give me that scrunchy.' She pointed to the scrunchy that Elsie wore constantly, on her wrist whenever it wasn't in her hair. Elsie handed it to her, and Rorie slipped it on her own wrist. Then Elsie stood right up close to Rorie and stared at her, as had become her habit when Rorie was transforming.

Rorie found herself shutting her eyes again; she couldn't bear the suspense. Quite apart from which, she now had to get used to the idea of taking on *Elsie* characteristics...bleugh!

She didn't have to wait very long. 'There!' cried Elsie. 'You're disappearing inside your bathrobe!'

Rorie opened her eyes and looked at her feet; they seemed tiny. 'Oh boy, so I am!' She clamped her hands to her face as she consulted the mirror. Her cheeks were filling out as her lips and eyebrows were thinning. Her eyes seemed to grow closer together.

She yanked off the scrunchy and threw it to the ground. 'OK, that's enough!' she declared.

'Hey!' cried Elsie indignantly. 'I wasn't finished!'

'Sorry, Else,' said Rorie, turning away. 'I told you, it just kind of freaks me out! It's not that I mind being you...' *I mind being you!* she said to herself.

'That's not fair!' said Elsie crossly, as she tried desperately to force the scrunchy back onto Rorie's wrist. Rorie snatched her hand away, so Elsie tugged on her hair. 'Come on!'

'Ouch! Stop that, will you? I said no!'

'You'd better tidy up in here,' came Cammy's voice from behind her. 'Or Nolita's going to be very cross with you.'

73

Rorie froze. *Don't turn around.* 'Oh yes, don't worry, Cammy!' she called, hunching down on the bed so as to disguise her shrunkenness.

'OK,' said Cammy. 'You come down for dinner when you're ready.'

So that's all right then, thought Rorie to herself in bed that night. *I still have my secret weapon.* The thought spread a warm sensation through her body. Only now that she had been confronted with the possibility that this 'weapon' might be lost did she appreciate how much it meant to her. She hadn't realised just how reassuring it had been to know it was there in the background, like a loyal friend, ready to be called upon in time of need. It was as if her chameleon, Arthur Clarkson, lived on, remaining with her when so much else had been lost.

But there it remained, locked up inside her, not needed for now. Although there was a part of her that was screaming out to discover more about Nolita. Rorie still didn't entirely trust her...had she deflected their questions about Mum and Dad out of concern that they shouldn't distress themselves? Or was there some other reason? She *could* hire a private detective, couldn't she? Why ever not?

Rorie turned over and shut her eyes. *That's the trouble with you*, she told herself. *You have a problem with trust. Nolita is your friend, not your enemy.* And trust was very important; Nolita had said so, hadn't she? 'It ain't gonna work if you don't put your faith in me,' she'd told her and Elsie. 'That's real important, guys...'

Chapter 8
fluffycat & Co.

Two weeks later

'It's out with that tired old Retro-Future look!' commanded Nolita in her weekly blog. 'Electra Kandara looked so divine last night in this outfit – it's all about *accessories*, girls! Do not be seen without a hat and gloves! And what about those shoes and that bag! You know you *must* have these. Go get 'em!'

The clothing rails trundled in and out.

In Nolita's virtual chatroom, which was 'Strictly for Nolita's Closest Friends!', Rorie was welcomed to the group. Different members literally faded in and out of the colourful sitting room during the course of the conversation, looking as realistic as people did in Fashionworld. As this was a social forum, they tended to improve on their digital images, so everyone except

76

Rorie had rather pixie-like faces, impossibly tiny waists and fantastically long legs.

'Hey, everybody, Rorie's having Fabulosity lessons with Chinchilla,' said fluffycat.

'Great! What did you learn today, Rorie?" asked lovelite.

'Oh, you know. How not to eat party food, how to Be Beguiling...'

'How do you Be Beguiling?'

'It's sort of to do with pretending there's a lot more to you than there really is...'

'I reely want to know how to do that?' gasped fluffycat.

'Hey, Rorie, I saw your sister's website, *Elsie's Favorit Froxx*. Funky!' said lovelite.

'Oh, yeah...'

'Never mind that,' said papaya, just now appearing in the room. 'Is it true you met Paloma Vega, Rorie?'

'Um, yeah...'

'That is so not fair?' complained fluffycat. 'I've been modelling for Nolita for two years now, I'm Paloma's biggest fan, and I've never met her!'

The conversation then centred on How to Wear the Latest Hats, and Rorie got bored, so she discreetly faded out, unnoticed. Nobody asked Rorie about her mum and dad, although everyone knew about the situation. Rorie sensed that they were uncomfortable with the subject. In any case, there was nothing to report...

Another week later
'Ditch all those clunky bags and cumbersome hats!' commanded Nolita. 'Too much *stuff*! Watch Sascha Novitska arriving in London on Wednesday – such simple grace with those light-as-air sandals and flowing locks. The hair is the thing! If you don't have it, go get it! Implants are so quick and easy now, there's no reason not to!'

'Hey, Rorie. I saw you in that fashion show, I so wish I had hair like yours?' said fluffycat. 'Where'd you get it?'

'Oh, it's mine.'

'*All* yours?'

Rorie felt embarrassed. 'Yes, um... Hey, did anyone see that movie—'

'I heard the best place to go is Ferrara's,' suggested minkie-pinkie, butting in.

The rest of the conversation was about hair. Rorie faded out.

Another week later

'The trouble with hair,' declared Nolita, 'is that it's so much *work*. Am I right, girls? Well, I have good news for you. Here's Alice X, appearing on stage last night, and just see how she's turned that heavy-hair look literally on its head! Short, short, short – that's the way to go. And with skirts to match. And the colour! Orange, lime green, black-patent...this look will make a huge splash. Even if you've never rebelled against anything, you can look as if you have, with the Alice X look!'

The clothing rails trundled in and out.

There was still no news on Rorie and Elsie's parents.

Two weeks after that

'I'm Rorie's sister, Elsie,' said the tall young lady who looked like a Disney princess.

'Oh, hello, Elsie,' said fluffycat. 'Where's Rorie?'

'She's got a modelling job. Anyhow, I been telling her I wanna go in the chatroom for ages, so she let me. She said anyhow I probly have more in common with you, 'cause all you talk about is fashion.'

'Meaning what?' remarked lovelite. 'She thinks there's other, better stuff to talk about? Well you can tell your stuck-up sister she doesn't have to come back. Plus, I'm not being mean or anything, but it doesn't make any difference how you enhance your image – we know you're only seven. And we don't really do *kindergarten* talk.'

'Neither do I!' Elsie replied indignantly. 'I'm an expert on cloves. I got my own fashion label, you know!'

'Yes, honey,' said kewpiedoll, 'because *Auntie Nolita* set it up for you to play with. Don't go thinking you're *clever*, or anything.'

'Well, let me tell you something!' snapped Elsie. 'My mum'n'dad, they invented –' Elsie fell silent. She had a lump in her throat.

'Invented what?'

'Not telling now,' Elsie retorted.

Then she faded out.

'Hey, hon, you look down in the mouth,' remarked Nolita, as Elsie joined the others in the kitchen. 'What's the matter?'

'I went in the chatroom,' said Elsie. 'An' they were mean to me. They said I'm too little, even though I made myself big.'

'Oh, a little joshing is all part of the fun,' laughed

Nolita. 'Don't take any notice.' She took a call on her Shel. 'Yep! Hey, Paloma. Great...c'mon over, we'll discuss.'

Rorie was silent, listlessly pushing pasta around her plate. She wished that, just for once, they could have an ordinary evening without all these interruptions.

Nolita peered at her. 'Rorie?'

Rorie forced a smile. She didn't feel she could say anything bad about the chatroom girls; they *were* all friends or protégés of Nolita's. 'Oh, I'm OK. It's just that...'

The words 'Mum and Dad' hung thickly in the air between them, but nothing was said. Rorie didn't feel able to discuss it with Nolita. She knew she would only be told she was wishing her life away, and what could she say to that? That Nolita didn't know what it was like? No – the trouble was, she did.

'OK, hon, you look as if you could use a little cheering up,' said Nolita, hitting some buttons on her Shel. 'I'm topping up some Fashionworld credit here. You go on in there later and get what you like. Retail therapy!'

'No!' snapped Rorie, suddenly standing up and sending her fork clattering to the floor. 'I...I don't want retail therapy!' Seeing the shocked look on

Nolita's face, she felt her own face flush. 'I'm sorry...I really just don't want any more *stuff*. Stuff doesn't help!'

'Hey...Rorie, all I'm trying to do is—'

'What?' Rorie shrieked, now really quite shocked at herself. But she was helpless to resist. It was as if a tiny fragment had fallen from the facade she'd developed and now the whole thing was crumbling. 'What *are* you trying to do? What do you want with us? You never really spend time with us!'

'Rorie!' gasped Elsie. 'That's not true. Nolita takes us everywhere!'

'That's not what I'm talking about!' insisted Rorie, so fired up that nothing would hold her back now. 'All that letting us tag along, it doesn't count. *Really* spending time together is...doing nothing in particular! Sunday afternoons in the park, stuff like that! Just ordinary stuff...' Her voice trailed away, as she remembered all the Sunday afternoons in the park with Mum and Dad. The words thickened in her throat. 'What *do* you want with us?' she asked Nolita again, her eyes glassy with tears. 'And why aren't you doing something about finding Mum and Dad?'

Nolita's face was hard. 'I can't help my lifestyle, Rorie. You knew from the start that I was a busy woman. That ain't about to change.' She sighed, as she reached down to pick up the fork. 'As for your parents, I have helped, by publicising the story. I can't do any more. Well, I guess this is what getting to know each other is all about,' she added, putting the fork in the sink. 'I'll know from now on not to suggest retail therapy...'

'You still can for me!' Elsie piped up.

Nolita smiled faintly. 'Sure thing, hon.' Her eyes lowered and she dug her fingertips into her temples. 'I...I have a headache. Would you excuse me, girls?' And she left the room.

'Now look what you've gone and done!' snarled Elsie. 'After all she's done for us!'

Chapter 9
The Butterfly

Rorie marched off to her room, the fiery ball of anger and frustration inside her now cooling to a miserable lump that felt depressingly like guilt. *Am I becoming spoilt?* she wondered. Part of her still felt she ought to be grateful to Nolita for all she'd done for them. But 'retail therapy' really did seem to be her answer to everything, and Rorie was beginning to wonder how much longer she could go along with it all. She felt like a balloon being pumped up every day with thrills and excitement, all of which *felt* like happiness…but then, *ss-ss-ss*, it all seeped out again at the end of the day.

Why did *everything* make her feel guilty these days? A glance in the closet was a nagging reminder of all those never-worn outfits Nolita had bought her, while she went on wearing her shabby old slants and clogs every day. She found them reassuring, like a comfort blanket, but it was clear this was beginning to annoy Nolita. 'I just want to see you looking nice,' she would say. Rorie's shabby appearance had also prompted Chinchilla to fret – she had prescribed ten repetitions of 'I am fabulous', and night-time hypnotherapy, in an attempt to cure her of this most grave condition. Rorie hadn't bothered with it, which only made her feel guiltier.

She slumped down by the window, where the low sun filtered through the trees. Directly below the window was one of Nolita's towering muses, a big 'A'-shaped thing with colossal boots, striding forth, head held high. It reminded Rorie of Nolita herself, not least because of those boots. But it was also the pose: going forward, never looking back, gazing upward. Nolita always seemed to live just in the moment; it was as if the past didn't exist to her. Apart from the story about the disappearance of her father, Nolita had given nothing away about her past – and even then she had talked of the need to move on, never look back.

The anger returned. Why *couldn't* she discuss such an important thing as her parents' disappearance, for heaven's sake? That wasn't wallowing, it was just normal! Rorie wanted to be able to talk about how unbearable it was for her that time was expanding between her and her parents, seemingly sending them further and further away.

To her surprise, at that moment Nolita knocked and entered the room – though as it turned out, it wasn't for a heart-to-heart. 'Hey, Rorie, just heard from Inspector Dixon,' she said briskly. 'There's nothing to report about your parents,' she added quickly, 'he's just coming to visit, see how things are going. OK?'

Rorie bit her lip. 'OK.'

'I've cancelled a couple of engagements especially,' Nolita added, then swiftly retreated.

A few moments later, Elsie appeared. 'So what you gonna do, tell 'spector Dixon you don't like Nolita any more?'

Rorie frowned. 'I never said I didn't like her.'

'You're acting like you don't.'

'I just…she's just…oh!' Rorie sighed heavily. 'She's OK, all right? I just think she's…*wrong* about certain things. And there are things about her I really don't understand, if you must know.'

Elsie put her hands on her hips, aping Nolita. 'Well, you better learn.'

*

By the time Inspector Dixon appeared, Rorie had managed to calm down. What else was she going to do? This was her home for now, and it was still better than any other. She would have to present a united front. And in fact there was so much to tell him about her modelling assignments, the various celebrities they'd met and so on, that by the end of his visit she had cheered up a little.

But as Dixon was leaving, Nolita followed him outside, and the two of them carried on chatting. Rorie was suddenly consumed with curiosity. Elsie had gone off to do some 'designering', so Rorie was on her own. She went out through the side door and surreptitiously made her way to the statue nearest to Dixon and Nolita, just catching the tail end of a conversation about a film starring Dixon's favourite actress, Iva Pasquale.

'...You'll love it, her best role yet,' Nolita was saying.

'Can't wait,' said Dixon. 'Well, best be on my way... Listen, there's one thing I ought to mention, didn't want to say it in front of the girls, but...well, we're scaling back the investigation into their parents' disappearance.'

Rorie didn't hear Nolita's response – she was too

busy keeping herself from crying out, hand clamped to her mouth.

'...There's only so long we can continue putting so many resources into something that's looking less and less likely to reap any reward,' Dixon went on.

'Of course,' said Nolita.

Rorie thought she might faint on the spot.

'That's not to say we've given up, of course,' Dixon added. 'But it's important that the girls can now build on what they have, prepare for the future...we have to recognise that their parents may never return.'

'They're not really going to, are they, Inspector?' said Nolita – a little too readily, Rorie thought.

'It's looking less and less likely,' said Dixon.

Rorie stood, frozen, still hunched against the statue as they said their goodbyes and parted. She watched as a butterfly landed on a flower nearby. It was unlike any other she'd seen before, with wings the size of beech leaves reflecting the sun with astonishing, iridescent blues. It reminded Rorie of what Dad had once said, likening his way of working to following a butterfly. 'I get a *hunch* about something,' he'd said, 'and I have to follow it...I'd go crazy if I didn't.' Rorie had more than just a hunch that her parents were still alive. She didn't know why, but she just *knew* they were. So, if they were still alive, and not suffering from amnesia (which Rorie had never truly thought possible anyway), then the only explanation left was that they had, as Elsie had suggested, been kidnapped. But who else was going to believe that? Not Nolita, not Inspector Dixon. And it was clear that Nolita wasn't going to head up any sort of special investigation of her own.

Follow the butterfly, said a voice in Rorie's head. *You'll go crazy if you don't.* She resolved there and then to find out as much as she could by herself about what had happened to Mum and Dad.

Just two days later, Rorie found herself sitting alone behind Nolita's desk, with the whole office to herself. True to her never-look-back style, Nolita had quickly forgotten her disagreement with Rorie, and by Monday morning was quite as upbeat as ever. Then she was called away on a celebrity wardrobe crisis. 'I tell you what you can do, hon,' she'd told Rorie. 'Since Artie's had to step out, could you stick around here and hold the fort for me?'

Rorie suddenly felt quite important. 'Oh, right... yeah, OK,' she said, trying to sound nonchalant.

'Artie'll be back around eleven,' said Nolita,

packing up her things. 'Meanwhile I'll direct network calls to the answering service. Here, I'll leave the Collection open; I'm expecting a delivery.'

And off she went.

So here was Rorie, alone in the office during a rare quiet moment, with Artie gone for at least another half an hour. What a chance to do some snooping! She twirled in the seat, thinking what a shame it was that the computer was switched off... There was little else worth looking at – just a few ebooks, doodle pads and fabric swatches on the desk. Nothing personal. Rorie had of course looked up public information on Nolita before – that was easy to do on her own Shel. But all she'd found was a lot of stuff she knew already. She tried the drawers. What she was burning to find out was whether Nolita knew something about her parents' disappearance that she wasn't letting on, especially after the way she'd spoken about it to Inspector Dixon on Saturday. For that matter, she might also find some answers as to why Nolita had been so quick to take in her and Elsie.

But there was nothing of interest in the drawers either. No, it had to be the computer. And as her gaze fell on the open Collection door, she suddenly knew exactly what to do.

Chapter 10
The Changing Picture Dress

Rorie's face lit up, literally. Glowing back at her was the Changing Picture Dress, now displaying a cascade of roses on a white background. Fumbling with excitement, she put it on.

It took only seconds for her to know that something was happening. In no time at all, she was consumed by that sickly, panicky sensation she always got whenever she was forced to let go of herself and assume another identity. She distracted herself by looking at Nolita's Power Boot collection. She decided to put on a pair for good measure. As she tried them on, she could see how her hands and feet were becoming scrawnier and veinier. Finally, she braced herself and looked in the mirror. Crinkles were appearing around her eyes, which had taken on a greenish tinge; hollows formed beneath her cheekbones, and her jawline went from oval to square. Her muscles grew more clearly defined, and her hair became thinner, straighter and redder – though not as short as Nolita's. Rorie inspected her teeth: no diamond. The transformation couldn't quite stretch to that.

She hurried back to the desk and powered up the big screen on the wall. 'Please say your name,' said the computer: the voice recognition test. 'Nolita,' Rorie answered, slightly taken aback at her suddenly very adult, New York-accented voice.

The screen displayed a moving-block graphic while it processed the voice attributes. Rorie chewed on her lip.

'Good morning, Nolita,' it said at last. 'Please place your thumb on the biopad.'

Oops, thought Rorie. *Now what?* There was no way her thumbprint was going to match Nolita's; the transformations were never that complete. So far, what she had ended up with was a sort of in-betweeny appearance, always with a bit of Rorie still evident. And before now, she had never experimented with ways of increasing the chameleon effect to see if she could make it work more completely – she'd never wanted to! More clothes, perhaps? No. Not in Nolita's case anyway – Rorie had already discovered how most of her wardrobe came and went too fast to have any effect.

She stared at her thumb. But what if she could somehow *concentrate* all the Nolita-ness into one part of her body? Right now, it made no difference what shape the rest of her was in – it was only the thumbprint that mattered. She picked up a pen that was lying on the desk. It was a special one, Rorie knew, and she had seen Nolita use it a lot. She *supposed* that objects were capable of having the same effect as clothing, but couldn't be certain. She pulled out a drawer. Inside was a bag of cosmetics, and in it was a well-used hairbrush, full of actual hairs from Nolita's head. Those had to be more potent still than clothing, surely?

Rorie hesitated. *Am I crazy?* she thought. This was really getting a bit weird. She stared at the screen, and contemplated giving up. But she was desperate; if not now, then when? And what was the worst that could happen if it didn't work? With a jarring sensation, she suddenly realised that it might set off some sort of alarm... *Well, I don't care!* she decided. This was too good a chance to miss.

She pulled a wad of hairs from the hairbrush and wrapped it around her right thumb. She took up the pen in the same hand, then pressed her hand against the fabric of the dress and shut her eyes. She focused all her mental energy onto her right thumb, while at the same time thinking of Nolita. She sat like that for a minute or more, not moving a muscle.

Finally, without having a clue whether it had worked or not – and in any case having no way of checking – she pressed her thumb on the biopad.

Once again, the moving-block graphics appeared. While Rorie waited, she consulted Nolita's mirror. She gasped. Her face, which had apparently completely changed back to 'Rorie', was now, faster than ever, returning to 'Nolita-Rorie' mode.

'*Thank you.*'

'Aahh!' cried Rorie, jumping at the voice of the computer. She turned to see Nolita's file icons appearing on the screen. Incredibly, it had worked. Rorie suddenly felt immensely powerful.

There was an icon marked simply 'Documents'. She tapped its image on the control panel. Two folders appeared, one marked 'Business', the other 'Personal'. Rorie clicked on 'Personal', which prompted a list of files to appear. They were listed alphabetically. Rorie scrolled down them to 'R', where she soon found 'Rorie'. But there was very little here; just some legal documents relating to the modelling work and the temporary care of herself and Elsie. Nothing about Mum and Dad.

Time was running out.

The back of her neck damp with sweat, Rorie tried the other 'Personal' files, but even as she did so she knew there would be little in them, because Nolita didn't have a life outside of work. *Work is play, and play is work*, as she had said. Which left the business files: *lots* of them.

And one stood out among all the others – one with a name that sent an electric charge straight to Rorie's heart: Rexco.

'*We're going up to London to present this to Rexco*,' echoed Dad's voice in her head. *What did Nolita have to do with Rexco?* wondered Rorie, suddenly quite nauseous. She clicked on the folder to open it, but no sooner had she done it than she heard sounds coming from reception. Artie must have come back early! Not that early, in fact; it was already ten to eleven. She knew she should shut everything down right away – but she couldn't, not now. She decided to take a gamble; there was a good chance Artie would just stay in reception and not come into the office.

She turned back to the screen.

The folder had revealed its contents: several files, each one entitled 'Rexco Sales' followed by the year. Rorie clicked on the most recent one. Then the door opened, and in walked Artie.

Panicked, Rorie dropped down behind the desk.

'Hi, Nolita,' said Artie. 'Hey, what are you doing down there?'

'Nothing!' snapped Rorie, sounding more shrill than she meant to. 'I mean, I just...dropped something.' Her voice sounded reassuringly Nolita-like, but as she crouched there in the glowing dress and funky boots, her heart was in her throat. He mustn't get any closer! She would have to stall him somehow – not only did she look more like Nolita's younger sister than Nolita herself, but they were dressed differently. Even someone who changed outfits frequently was hardly likely to put something on for just a few minutes, and the real Nolita would soon appear in what she had been wearing before.

Rorie risked a quick glance over the top of the desk. 'Get me a coffee, will you, hon?' she managed, doing her best to sound casual. 'I'm gasping!'

'OK,' said Artie. 'Where's Rorie? In the Collection?'

Rorie-as-Nolita risked one more peep above the precipice. 'Oh, don't...uh, go in there, she's...

96

changing.' *Well, that's truer than you know*, she thought to herself.

'Rorie? You want anything?' Artie called in the direction of the changing room.

'Oh, no that's fine, Artie,' Rorie answered hurriedly. 'She just...had an iced tea a little while ago...ah! Found it,' she added, aware that she'd been crouched behind the desk for rather longer than seemed feasible, and taking the chance that Artie was on his way out to get the coffee anyway.

'Oh, good,' said Artie, and – at last! – left the room.

Rorie stood up and smoothed the dress down. Shaking, she reached for the control panel, intending to shut down – but first she just *had* to get a quick look at that Rexco document which was now open on the screen. While one half of her brain mapped out the imagined actions of Artie as he went about getting 'Nolita' a coffee, tracking his progress, the other half scanned the sales document.

The first thing that struck her was the logo at the top; she knew it from somewhere, but couldn't quite place it. The document was three pages long, and consisted mostly of graphs and charts. Almost dizzy with impatience, Rorie did her best to drink in all she could, and to make some sense of it. Store names – lots of them. Famous ones, and all owned, it showed here, by Rexco. *Good grief!* she thought. *They own all of them?*

Artie would be heading to the kitchen by now – no, he would have got someone else to go. Good. More delay...

BJ Slaxx, The Rap...they were all here. Even some very fancy designer names like Moochie and Dada... all owned by Rexco. Then there were some other names that meant nothing to her, apparently other kinds of businesses...something called Tramlawn sounded familiar...

I have to stop! Rorie told herself. Trembling, she wiped the sweat from her brow. *No! Just one moment longer...* Graphs, charts... Here...here was Nolita's name. A pie chart – a wheel of cheese showing how ownership of Rexco was divided up – on one stonking great wedge of it was Nolita's name.

Go now! her insides screamed. *Get out before it's too late!*

Her head reeling, she quickly shut the computer down. She could hear Artie's footsteps approaching. She dived across the office and into the Collection.

There was the sound of Artie crossing the floor, then placing the coffee mug on the desk. 'Nolita?'

'I'm...just changing,' Rorie called out.

'Coffee's on your desk, OK?'

'Thanks!' Rorie listened to Artie retreat, then leant against the wall and heaved a sigh of relief. Her mind was a jumble of names, graphs and pie charts, and she struggled to get to grips with all the information. She wished she had had more time to look at the information on the screen...but she was still in the Changing Picture Dress, so she still had access to Nolita's knowledge, didn't she? Surely she could just hold the question in her head, *what does it all mean?* and 'Nolita' would have the answers. Rorie tried it. She tried really hard, emptying her mind of all Rorie-ness as much as she could. But the torrent of information was not forthcoming. She was discovering the limits of her chameleon changes; it really was only where actions were involved that they had any effect. She switched to thinking about the Rexco logo – where *had* she seen it before?

She found herself pacing up and down, deep in thought. So deep in fact, that she didn't hear the approaching footsteps. By the time she heard the swish of the Collection door, it was too late to hide. She came face to face with Nolita.

Chapter 11
Big Cheese

The two Nolitas stared at each other, stunned.

Nolita number one flipped open her Shel. 'My God, what is this? Emergency, we have an intruder!' An alarm sounded almost immediately.

Rorie stepped forward. 'Nolita, I can explain—'

'You stay away from me!' shrieked Nolita, grabbing hold of a nearby chair and holding it up in self-defence. 'I've heard about crazies like you, stalking your idols…having surgery to look like them. How did you get in here? Impersonating me, I suppose?'

'No, no, no!' yelled Rorie over the din of the alarm. 'I was here already. It's me: Rorie.'

Nolita shook the chair. 'Aargh! You even sound like me!'

'Didn't you hear what I said? It's me, Rorie.'

Nolita peered from behind the chair, her eyes like

green ice. 'No, that's crazy. What do you *mean*, you're Rorie?'

'You left me here to hold the fort while you and Artie were out,' Rorie yelled over the din. 'Those were your words: "hold the fort". You left the Collection doors open because you were expecting a delivery.'

'You'd know all that if you were an intruder who'd already got in.'

'OK...' Rorie thought, then clicked her fingers. 'Your dad. He disappeared when you were seven years old, when he went out for a can of Spray-Fix. You told me and Elsie all about it, and how we shouldn't wish our lives away... *Please*, Nolita. Just call off the alarm, and let me change back into my own clothes. Then I'll explain.'

Nolita put the chair down. She stepped forward, peering more closely. Rorie squirmed under the scrutiny; she felt as if it was written all over her face that she'd been snooping in Nolita's files. *But she can't possibly know*, she reminded herself. Nolita took hold of her arm. 'I don't get this, but...you do kind of *look* like Rorie.'

'That's because I *am* Rorie!'

At that moment, two large men burst into the room. To Rorie's relief, Nolita held up her hand.

'It's OK, guys, she's meant to be here. She just...took me by surprise.'

'You sure?' said one of the men.

'Yes, I'm sure. Please shut off the alarm.'

The men stood there, looking confused.

'Well, go on!'

'Yes, ma'am,' they replied at last, and retreated.

Nolita looked Rorie over again. 'This is weird. What are you doing in my clothes?'

The inside of Rorie's mouth felt like sandpaper. 'That's what changes me. But I never meant...y-you came back so s-soon... Look, I need to change back. Please!'

Nolita slowly let go of her arm, and Rorie fled behind the clothing racks. Trembling, she undid the Changing Picture Dress, kicked off the Power Boots and pulled on her top and slants. She leant against the wall and took some deep breaths. *Calm down!* she told herself. *She doesn't have to know* everything...

'Rorie?' called Nolita.

'Yes, yes, I'm coming.' Glancing at her reflection in the mirror, she headed back.

'...I just wanted to see what it was like being you,' said Rorie, concluding her explanation. While they'd been sitting together she had gradually been changing, and was now completely back to her normal appearance. She had told Nolita how it had all happened as a result of being struck by lightning with Arthur Clarkson, and how she had disguised herself as Aunt Irmine to escape from Poker Bute Hall. What she didn't tell her was the part about how she was able to pick up knowledge from her subject as well... She could only hope and pray that Artie wouldn't say anything about the fact that the computer had been on when he'd come into the room. There wasn't necessarily any reason to do so; for all he knew, it had never been switched off.

Nolita had been silent throughout the explanation. 'Wow,' she said at last. 'That is...wow. I never heard of such a thing. Can that really happen? I mean, I guess it can – you're living proof! Who knows about this?'

Rorie felt a renewed swell of panic. 'It's really secret – *please* don't tell anyone! Oh, but...did Artie see you just now?'

'Artie?' said Nolita. 'Is he back?'

Rorie heaved a sigh of relief. 'Then Elsie's the only other person who knows.'

'You didn't tell *me*.' Nolita's face was stony.

'Well, I –'

'Remember what we agreed, Rorie,' said Nolita. 'Complete trust, right?'

Rorie stared at her hands. She thought back to the conversation they'd had when Nolita had first offered to take in her and Elsie. She remembered being struck by the intensity of Nolita's stare as she'd emphasised her point about needing complete trust. '*It ain't gonna work otherwise*,' she'd warned them. Looking back, Rorie now saw this in a new light; had Nolita said it because she had something to hide?

'Are there any other secrets you wanna tell me?' Nolita's gaze pierced right through her.

'No!' said Rorie quickly, immediately realising with a hot, giddy sensation that this was it – if her other secret ever came out now, she would really be in trouble. 'There's nothing else, I promise.'

That evening, as Rorie lay in her bed mulling everything over, the image of the Rexco logo hovered in her mind's eye once again. Where had she seen it before?

She found herself picturing it on a desk – some sort of puzzle, an 'executive toy'... Then she realised *whose* desk it had been on: Uncle Harris's, back in his headmaster's office at Poker Bute Hall. The puzzle had been right next to the vulture-in-a-meringue wedding picture of Aunt Irmine. Made out of interlocking Perspex shapes which seemed to be abstract at first, she had eventually identified the 'R' and the 'X'. As soon as she realised this, she also remembered where she had seen the word 'Tramlawn': Poker Bute Hall was owned by a company called 'Tramlawn Schools'.

Rorie suddenly felt as if she had swallowed something poisonous. She sat bolt upright in bed. 'Psst! Elsie!'

'Mnnmm,' mumbled Elsie, turning over sleepily.

Rorie went to Elsie's bedside and gently shook her shoulder. 'Elsie, something's happened.'

Elsie sat up quickly and stared woozily at her. 'What?'

'I got into Nolita's files, and I've found out some stuff.'

Elsie perked up. 'Hey, how'd you do that?'

Rorie shook her head. 'Never mind. Look, I'm worried about Rexco.'

'Rexco?'

'There's all these connections, and...look, from what I can tell, Nolita basically has a major stake in the business.'

Elsie looked puzzled. 'A *steak*?'

'I mean...she owns part of it.'

'No! Really?'

'Yes.'

'Wow, what a coinstance!'

Rorie regarded Elsie doubtfully. It was clear that as far as she was concerned, Nolita could do no wrong. 'OK, well…why do you suppose she'd have kept so quiet about that?'

Elsie shrugged, then frowned. 'Are you sure?'

'Yes! And you know what else? Rexco own Tramlawn Schools, and Tramlawn, if you remember, is the company that runs Poker Bute Hall.'

'So that means Uncle Harris…'

'…Works for Rexco. Effectively. Oh, Elsie, it feels like they're everywhere! Is there nothing they don't control?'

'Well, there's shops…'

'Oh! Those too.'

'The shops?'

'Yup. A lot of them, anyway.'

'Wow. How can anyone be that rich?'

'I don't know.'

Elsie flopped back on her pillow. 'Wow. Imagine what it would be like to own the who-o-ole world! Freaky.'

Rorie sighed. 'Elsie, you don't get it, do you? I'm

beginning to wonder if...well, if you didn't have a point. When you suggested that maybe Rexco kidnapped Mum and Dad.'

Elsie flipped over again. 'Really? Well, then we'd better tell Inspector Dixon!'

'I...well...' Rorie paused. What could she really say to Dixon? It all pressed in on her, feeling as if it meant something, but when it came down to it, what evidence did she have that Rexco were involved in a kidnapping? None. Nothing more than a hunch. And how would she explain how she came to know what she did, anyway?

'No, we can't say anything,' she said finally. 'At least...not yet. He wouldn't believe us. Look, I'll work on it, OK?'

'Why don't we ask Nolita about Rexco?' suggested Elsie.

'No!' Rorie was beginning to wish she hadn't said anything. 'I mean...OK, *I'll* ask her. But not yet; in a couple of days. Otherwise Nolita might connect it with what happened today, and get suspicious.'

As it turned out, Nolita had to go to Rome until the end of the week anyway. Rorie found herself obsessively surfing the web for information about Rexco, but, as with Nolita, only ever came across a fraction of what she already knew; very general information, like the address of their main headquarters in New York, and the names of just three companies they owned, as opposed to the dozens she'd seen listed on Nolita's computer. *What exactly am I looking for anyway?* she wondered. She didn't really know, but she couldn't get the idea out of her head that there was something significant about Uncle Harris and Aunt Irmine's apparent connection to them, and Nolita's very obvious involvement. Another spying session was out of the question; it would be disastrous for her to be seen in her 'Nolita' guise while Nolita herself was Rome. So Rorie waited patiently for her return, the thoughts chasing each other in circles in her head.

'Your sister is just *desperate* to come away with me on my next trip,' laughed Nolita, when she and Rorie were finally alone together in the kitchen at the weekend. Elsie, having seemingly forgotten all about Nolita's connection to Rexco, had been bombarding her with questions about the Rome trip, before disappearing off to play.

'She doesn't understand that they're not holidays,' said Rorie.

'Well,' said Nolita, studying her Shel as she poured herself some seaweed juice. 'There's that shoot you're involved with in Cornwall next Thursday. I'm going too, meeting with some designers down there. I guess Elsie could come along to that. Not as glamorous as Rome, I know, but...'

'Nolita, I've been thinking,' Rorie ventured. 'Do you remember I said that our mum and dad had an appointment with a company called Rexco the day they went, uh...missing?'

Nolita didn't take her eyes off her Shel. 'Mm-hmm...?'

'Well, I just, uh, wondered if you knew anything about them?'

Nolita glanced up from her Shel, her green eyes unfocused.

'Rexco,' Rorie repeated. 'Do you know anything about them?'

Nolita shook her head. 'Not sure I do – oh wait, it's some sort of scientific organisation, right?'

Rorie was stunned. Suddenly her mouth went dry again and words shrivelled up like burnt bits of paper. Whatever reaction she had expected from Nolita, it wasn't this. 'Um...yeah.' She cleared her throat, as she struggled to frame another question. 'Only I think they might be involved in other stuff too,' she managed at last. 'Like, uh…clothing stores?'

Nolita shrugged. 'Could be. I wouldn't be surprised. Lots of—' At that moment she got a call on her Shel, and that was the end of the discussion.

Rorie left the room, her face burning. As she headed up to her room, she replayed the conversation over and over again in her mind. Nolita's blank, expressionless look; how effortless it had been. How easily she had lied. And it *was* a lie – no doubt about it. File after file of records, right there on her computer, saying Rexco, Rexco, Rexco. And there was her name on the pie chart: Nolita Newbuck, big cheese. Big fat chunk of Gorgonzola, right there. Rorie had seen it with her own eyes.

And it stank.

Chapter 12
Pandora's Box

Rorie felt as if she would burst. She would have to talk to Inspector Dixon now – she would go crazy if she didn't. But how would she be able to see him in private? She wasn't allowed out alone – Nolita insisted that she be accompanied by one of her security team unless she was with another trusted adult. She was stumped.

But when, a couple of days later, Tinky mentioned she was going shopping for a wedding outfit on her way home, Rorie quickly volunteered to go with her. 'Tell Nolita I just stepped out with Tink for a bit,' she told Cammy, linking arms with Tinky. 'Might do some shopping myself!'

'Shopping!' exclaimed Cammy. 'You've got Fashionworld, what do you need with a dirty, crowded shop full of the smell of other people's feet?'

'Oh, sometimes it's just nice to go in a *real* shop,' insisted Rorie.

Rorie chatted fast and furiously with Tink as they shopped, getting her carried away as they discussed the wedding she was going to. Just as Rorie had hoped, Tink became thoroughly wrapped up in the subject. 'Ooh, I can't wait!' she squealed as she emerged from the store, pristine glossy carrier bag hanging from her arm. 'It is going to be *so* romantic!'

And as Rorie had hoped, Tinky wound up running late. 'Blimey, is that the time?' she gasped, glancing at her Shel. 'I'll never catch the 6.45! Come on, let's get you home.'

'Oh, it's fine, Tink,' said Rorie. 'I know the way, I'll be OK – you go.'

'No way!' insisted Tink, taking her arm and speeding up. 'You know the rules. Come on.'

They hurried on until they came to Nolita's house. 'Thanks, Tink, I'll be fine now,' said Rorie, as she approached the entrance. 'Off you go!'

'OK, love. Bye!'

As soon as Tinky's curly head bobbed out of sight, Rorie turned and headed for the solartram, heart pounding. Lurching across the river on the crowded tram, she was gripped by the same horrible, sickly feeling she had felt earlier that day when Nolita had lied about Rexco; only now it was magnified tenfold.

All the images did a circular dance in Rorie's head: the Perspex shapes on Uncle Harris's desk, the pie chart, Nolita's blank look...round and round they flew, like the nasty and evil spirits unleashed from the famous mythical box Pandora opened when she knew she wasn't supposed to. A phrase Rorie had heard somewhere popped into her head: 'What you don't know can't hurt you.' *How silly was that!* she thought, as she walked into the police station. *Of course it could.*

'I want to see Inspector Dixon, please,' she announced breathlessly at the enquiries desk. 'My name's Rorie Silk.'

The young officer at the desk blew his nose dispassionately. 'Is he expecting you?'

'Well, no – not exactly...but I must speak with him, it's really important!'

The officer regarded her with weary, red-rimmed eyes. 'I'm afraid, if you haven't got an appointment, I can't really—'

'*Please*,' insisted Rorie. 'I have some important information. It's to do with the disappearance of my parents, Arran and Laura Silk.' Her voice wobbling,

Rorie just managed to add, 'Inspector Dixon's leading the investigation.'

Without replying, the officer sighed and pressed a button in front of him. He sniffed. 'A Rorie Silk wishes to speak with you, sir. Says she's got some information.'

Rorie felt a little shot of excitement, or dread, as he instructed her to wait. A few moments later, Dixon appeared and strode over to her, beaming. 'Well, well, now, this is a surprise. How are you, Rorie?'

'Um, OK,' said Rorie awkwardly.

'How's Iva Pasquale?' asked Dixon jovially, as they headed over to his office.

'I don't know,' Rorie mumbled.

Dixon shut the door and indicated for Rorie to sit down. 'All right, Rorie, I can see something's troubling you,' he said, serious now. 'What's up?'

Rorie, swallowed hard. She fell silent, not knowing where to start. 'Oh, Inspector Dixon, I think there's something terrible going on!' she blurted out at last. She took a deep breath. 'I'm sorry, but I –'

'It's all right, Rorie,' said Dixon, fixing her with a firm gaze now. 'Take your time.'

'Oh, Inspector! I know you don't think you're going to find Mum and Dad...I–I heard you talking to

Nolita about cutting back on the search.'

Inspector Dixon's eyebrows rose. 'Ah. Well, you know it doesn't mean—'

'I know it doesn't mean you've given up,' Rorie interrupted quickly, 'but you have to know that there's more to all this than meets the eye. A lot more! Look, this may sound silly to you, but I've been thinking, and...I know you said it wasn't very likely, but I believe Elsie might have been onto something after all when she talked about Rexco having Mum and Dad kidnapped!' It was not until she uttered these words that they took on an air of alarming reality, and she found herself trembling.

Dixon furrowed his brow. 'Rorie, I really don't think—'

'That invention of Mum and Dad's was important,' interrupted Rorie. '*Really* important, worth millions!'

'Well, yes Rorie, we've been over this,' said Dixon. 'But you're saying nothing new has come to light? Nothing at all?'

Rorie felt the sweat beading up around her temples, in spite of the air conditioning. She couldn't let on about how she'd found out what she knew. 'No, but...look, can we just *suppose* for a minute...' She stood up and began pacing back and forth. 'Suppose

Mum and Dad really *did* get to Rexco, and that man who called our home asking for them was just *pretending* they hadn't...I've been thinking a lot about this, Inspector, and it all fits, it really does! I think they're holding them prisoner because, well, people do bad things when there's millions involved! Also Uncle Harris *hates* my dad, and he's in on it too—'

'Rorie—'

'No, please listen!' Rorie gulped hard. 'Rexco own some other company which runs schools, including Poker Bute Hall. And Uncle Harris has this thing on his desk, with the Rexco logo—'

'Hold on, hold on,' said Dixon, raising his hands. 'Look, I'm sorry you've got yourself worked up into a state, Rorie. But you're letting your imagination run away with you. OK, let's imagine for argument's sake that Rexco are these big evil baddies. Well, there's no point in kidnapping someone unless you're holding them to ransom, and there is no third party here that Rexco would be trying to extract a ransom from. Do you see?'

'But—'

'And if for some reason it was the *inventions* that were the problem,' Dixon went on, 'and Rexco wanted to make sure that they never saw the light of day, well, in that case...looking at this purely from a criminal point of view, you understand, and not from any realistic point of view of a respectable corporation...well, the motive would exist to – pardon me, Rorie...to kill them.'

'Oh no, but they couldn't, you see,' said Rorie quickly. 'Because they'd need Mum and Dad's help, developing the inventions. But then? When the work's all done? *Then* they kill them.' Rorie swallowed hard. 'Look, even Nolita is connected to Rexco, and she won't admit it. Why would she lie about that, if there wasn't something bad to hide?'

'Rorie, Nolita's a highly successful businesswoman – it's up to her what she chooses to be discreet about. Obviously, if we had evidence to suggest she'd been involved in something suspect, we'd question her. But we don't.'

Rorie stared at him, her face aflame. Every jigsaw piece that had fallen so neatly into place was now being yanked away by Inspector Dixon, as he systematically demolished the picture she'd built up. 'Why can't you understand?' she shrieked. *Get a grip*, she told herself, squeezing her knuckles. 'Look, maybe there's some other explanation for all of this,' she tried, more calmly. 'But what if I'm right? My mum and dad are in *danger*, I can feel it in my bones! And time's running out, Inspector. It's already been over two months – *something needs to be done!*' She practically shrieked these last words.

Dixon stood up. 'All right, Rorie...take it easy now,' he said, in a soft, soothing voice. He got up, went to the water cooler and filled a cup. 'Here, drink this.'

Rorie gratefully took the water and drank. Her hand trembled as she tipped back the cup.

'Believe me, I do understand what you're going through,' said Dixon. 'I've seen it time and again in people who have suffered great stress and anxiety. I assume Nolita doesn't know you're here?'

Rorie drained the last drop of water. 'No.' She checked her Shel; no messages. 'And she's not wondering where I am yet...'

'Look, I know you're upset, Rorie,' said Dixon softly. 'And I know how frustrating it must be when so much time passes and nothing seems to be happening. But I think you're putting two and two together and making twenty-seven.'

'But—'

'Please,' said Dixon firmly, with a pressing gesture of the hands. 'I promise you we are still doing everything possible to try to determine what happened to your parents. But we wouldn't investigate anyone at Rexco without a lot more behind us than a vague hunch. *But,*' he added, just as Rorie opened her mouth to say something, 'your statement will be kept on file. Should we uncover anything suspicious at all, I promise we will act accordingly.'

Rorie stared at her hands.

'I'll give you a ride back,' suggested Dixon. 'We can talk on the way. Don't worry, I won't go up the drive; Nolita won't know that you've been out.'

Chapter 13
Ballgown and Clogs

'Where were you?' demanded Elsie. 'You've been gone *ages*.'

Rorie looked around. 'Where's Nolita?'

'She had to go out,' said Elsie. 'So?'

'I told you; I was with Tink.'

'D'ya buy anything?'

'No.'

'So what took you so long then?'

'I was just *looking*, OK?' snapped Rorie. 'Good grief, why don't you just leave me alone?' She stormed off upstairs in a stew of emotions. She couldn't see any point in telling Elsie about her visit to Inspector Dixon. What good would it do? She had been made to look a fool. Yet despite Dixon's attempts to quell her alarm, she didn't feel in the least bit reassured. The nagging feeling that her parents were alive somewhere, and in deep trouble, just wouldn't go away. It kept on gnawing away at her insides. The image of Great-Grandma's saggy-jowled face would appear before her, those watery red-rimmed eyes piercing her as she said, 'You'll find them, you know. You will!'

For the umpteenth time, Rorie looked up Rexco on her Shel; although it got her precisely nowhere, it made her feel as if she were doing something positive. She could never find anything new, no matter how hard she tried; just those same three faceless companies they owned, the headquarters in New York...

Feeling guilty for snapping at Elsie, she went to find her. Predictably, Elsie was in the virtual reality room, lost in Fashionworld. Rorie went to join her, surprising her in the Paper Doll section. Together they messed around – for how long Rorie couldn't tell, but it did her a power of good, and she quite forgot about her worries. She designed a truly outrageous outfit, put it on, and was sailing down the catwalk when all of a sudden she stumbled and fell off the side of the runway, spinning and tumbling as if she were hurtling through miles and miles of space, hitting nothing, seeing only a whizzing blur of colours. She flailed about trying to catch onto something, but there was just void.

Then came the words, 'You betrayed my trust!' and all of a sudden Rorie was back in the dimly lit cocoon of the virtual reality room, with a furious Nolita looking down at her.

'Wha…?' Rorie rubbed her eyes and shook her head as she tried to adjust, and then she realised what had happened. Nolita had disconnected the power to her chair and removed her headset. The falling sensation had been a result of the sudden withdrawal from virtual reality.

'How did you get into my personal files?' demanded Nolita. Her eyes seemed greener, like two intense emeralds.

Rorie was stunned. 'I…er…'

'I know you did, so don't try to lie to me,' said Nolita. She stood with hands on hips, her bare arms sticking out like jug handles either side of her.

Elsie sat up in her seat and stared, bewildered.

'I'm sorry,' said Rorie, her mind flailing around wildly. 'I…was just playing a game, pretending to be you; I didn't really look at anything…'

'*How did you get into my files?*' Nolita repeated. 'I've just been on the office computer for the first time since Monday, when you were there by yourself. Whoever logged on last did not log off before shutting down, and I *always* log off!'

'Well...' Rorie hesitated. She was about to explain that she had of course been able to pass the voice recognition test, but then she remembered the biopad. She couldn't let on about that! She would have to think up some other explanation – and quickly. *Think, think!*

Nolita stood there, waiting.

'The computer...' Rorie fumbled around. She remembered one time when she had looked at some things on Mum's computer when she wasn't supposed to...how had she done that? Ah, yes... 'The computer was on already,' she said at last.

'No, it wasn't,' said Nolita. 'I shut down before I left. I *always* shut down.'

'I think what happened is, there was one application which failed to quit,' suggested Rorie. 'Maybe you were in a hurry, and didn't wait around to see if everything quit?'

Nolita frowned. 'Well, I don't think –'

'Because I found it in sleep mode,' Rorie lied, capitalising on Nolita's uncertainty. 'It just started right up when I touched the keyboard. All I looked at was fashions and stuff –'

Nolita stared at her. 'I don't believe you.'

Rorie felt the word 'Rexco' hanging in the air between them, although Nolita remained silent on that particular matter.

'Oh, Rorie always tells the truth!' protested Elsie. 'She doesn't make stuff up like me!'

'Yes, Nolita,' added Rorie, though the lying made her squirm inside. 'I promise, it's true!'

'I told you I needed you to put your faith in me!' Nolita was really raising her voice now. 'Nothing works without that! You've broken a bond; it's broken, broken...'

Elsie began to cry loudly.

Rorie was lost for words.

Nolita's eyes shone brightly. She sighed loudly, then shook her head. 'How could you?' she said quietly, then left the room.

Elsie howled like a pining dog; her face now resembled something that had been chewed up and spat out, all glistening and crumpled.

For twenty-four hours afterwards, Nolita didn't speak to Rorie or Elsie. She went on in her usual hyper-busy state, and the only difference was that she didn't include the girls in anything.

How long would things go on like this? Rorie had

no idea, but it was making her quite sick with anxiety. One moment she felt guilty for what she had done; the next, she was wracked with suspicion towards Nolita. And coursing through it all was a heightened sense of panic about Mum and Dad, her hunch that they were still alive as strong as ever...

By Sunday evening, Nolita had calmed down a bit, and came to see them. It wasn't exactly forgiveness – the hurried hug and the half-smile told Rorie that deep down Nolita was still wary of her. 'OK, hon, from now on I gotta have absolute trust,' said Nolita. 'Is that a deal?'

Rorie nodded gratefully, 'Yes, it's a deal.' But behind her back, her fingers were crossed; secretly she knew that yet another chapter in her life had closed.

'Else, we have to leave,' said Rorie later that night, after Nolita had gone out for the evening.

Elsie sat up in bed, distraught. 'But I thought everyfing was OK now!'

Rorie went and knelt on the floor in front of her. 'Well, it isn't. No, please don't start crying again. Look, have you completely forgotten what I told you about Nolita and Rexco?'

'No, but she wouldn't do anyfing bad, I know it.'

'Oh yeah?' said Rorie. 'Well, I asked her yesterday what she knew about Rexco, and she made out she had nothing to do with them. Why would she do that, Elsie?'

'But Nolita's *nice*!' insisted Elsie.

'She's…' Rorie broke off, unable to say what Nolita was. At first she had seemed so amazingly wonderful – on the fabulosity scale, she was off the charts. She was like a new invention of how a person could be. But *nice*? 'Fabulous' and 'nice' seemed to go together like a silk ballgown and old clogs, and they certainly didn't belong together under the same skin. But Elsie didn't understand this, and Rorie couldn't figure out how to explain it. So instead she moved on to explain her theory about what had happened to Mum and Dad, just as she had told it to Inspector Dixon.

Elsie's jaw fell open. 'You think they'll *kill* them?'

Rorie ran her fingers through her hair wearily. 'Look, I don't know anything for sure – how could I? All I know is that it's *possible*, and if we don't do something drastic, we'll never know. The longer we sit around here in la-la fashion-land not doing anything about it, the greater the risk that…that something awful will happen. I mean, for all we know they could have been moved by now, to New York or somewhere…'

'New York?'

'Rexco have their HQ there,' explained Rorie. 'Look, the point is, anything might have happened – we have to get out while there's a chance they're still alive!'

'But the police—'

'The police won't do anything! They think I'm crazy.'

Elsie gasped. 'Why? How'd you know?'

Rorie explained all about her visit to Inspector Dixon. 'Look, I've made my mind up about this, Else,' she concluded. 'I've got a gut feeling, and I need to go with that – just the way Dad used to with his inventions. Remember the way he used to liken the process to following a butterfly? That's what I need to do. And either you're in, or you're out. It's me, or Nolita.'

Chapter 14
The Sailing Hat

Rorie clutched her new designer backpack, nervously fingering the clasp as they hurtled down the hyperway in the limousine; she hadn't slept all night. Every now and then she would reach inside and pull out her hairbrush or take a sip from her water bottle, but these actions were just an excuse to check once again that yes, there were Nikki Deeds's trainers, Leesa Simms's cravat, Aunt Irmine's jacket and Moll's necklace. Her four secret weapons. One to give her fantastic athletic ability, one for technological know-how, one so she'd know how to drive a car and one for code-breaking. There, too, was her wallet, with its paydisc recently topped up from her hard-earned wages, as well as some cash she had saved up. The cash would soon run out, though, and she would have to use the paydisc quickly, before Nolita cancelled it, and only with a trader who was prepared to wipe the transaction for a fee, so that her movements couldn't be traced.

Fortunately, Nolita was her usual overworked self, completely absorbed in calls on her Shel, consulting files, making arrangements for the coming days, so Rorie really didn't think she had noticed her furtive checking.

Elsie was uncharacteristically quiet, especially as they were going on an outing, which would normally have had her behaving like an excitable puppy. Rorie wished Elsie could at least *act* as if she were excited, but realised that this would be like expecting a statue to spring to life. Poor Elsie. Rorie felt a twinge of guilt for presenting her with such a terrible choice; she knew that Nolita had virtually become the centre of Elsie's entire universe. But even a bond like that was not powerful enough to tear two sisters apart. And Rorie knew that Elsie, too, wanted to believe she could do something about Mum and Dad. No, this was how it had to be. Rorie was absolutely sure of that.

While Rorie pretended to read her ebook, she ran through the escape plan in her head. Because Nolita's home and office were heavily ringed with security people, Rorie had realised she stood a better chance of getting away undetected while out on a shoot. She also knew how chaotic these things could be. When they took a break, she would find somewhere to change, and transform herself. She had decided that the Leesa Simms guise was the best one because Leesa was squat, ugly and spotty, and therefore invisible to someone like Nolita. It might also have the added bonus of lending her the electronic know-how to start up an electric bike without a remote, should the need arise. As for Elsie, Rorie had the perfect thing: a black wig from Fashionworld, in a style that was bang up to date for under-tens everywhere. With the right clothes, Elsie would blend into the crowd within seconds.

The limousine drew up in car park No. 27 outside St Ives. With all the equipment transferred to trolleys, Nolita and her crew made their way out of the car park, past The Cornish Experience leisure and hotel complex, and on to the solartram stop, where they were transferred down into the bay.

'The whole town is closed to vehicles,' Nolita explained, which made Rorie uneasy; so much for any fast getaways.

'Oh, really?' said Elsie, casting a sidewards glance at Rorie. 'Why's that?'

'Has been ever since I can remember,' said Nolita.

'Used to get too congested. It's all narrow winding streets...such a cute place, real old. You'll like it.'

Rorie peered down at the warren of huddled streets below, a stark contrast from the biodomes and high-rise hotels of The Cornish Experience at the top of the hill. At least it looked as if it was easy to get lost in. She cast a glance at Elsie, but couldn't tell what she was thinking.

The cry of seagulls chased the wind. It was a bright, breezy summer's day. Rorie breathed in the salty air; she could almost taste freedom already. But as she went through the outfits with Tinky and the other two models, a heavy feeling of regret swept over her. She would miss Tink – she had become a real friend. Rorie shook the thought out of her head. *Don't think about the people you're going to miss*, she told herself. *Mum and Dad are more important than anything.*

Elsie sat nearby, legs swinging, apparently completely absorbed; watching the models parade up and down the harbour in their 'home-made artisan' clothes (next week's must-have look) was clearly providing a welcome distraction from what lay ahead.

And what, exactly, *did* lie ahead? Rorie tried not to think about it – it gave her butterflies in her belly. She would just have to figure things out as she went along. A growing crowd of holiday-makers surrounded them as they worked, something Rorie had learnt to ignore. She slipped into the routine, twirling her way along the stone pier that marked the divide between the picturesque old harbour and the much newer boating marina.

It felt like an eternity till it was time for a break, but at last it came. 'OK girls, half an hour,' said Mo, the photographer.

'I'm gasping for a cuppa tea,' said Tinky, approaching Rorie. 'You coming?'

'Yeah...in a minute. But I need to get out of this itchy outfit first. You go on ahead.'

Tink looked unsure for a moment, and Rorie thought she was going to insist on waiting. But the rest of the team had already left, including Nolita, who was busy talking on her Shel, and Tink gazed after them. 'Cor, I've got to get to the loo, an' all,' she said. 'OK, seeya in a bit.' She waved as she turned and headed towards the town.

Rorie waved back, and felt a stab of – what was it? Guilt? No, it was a strange mixture of feelings. Part of her hoped never to see Nolita again, yet at the same time the thought was sad and painful. She headed towards the changing tent, and the holiday-makers drifted away.

Then she noticed Elsie was gone. 'Elsie?' Rorie walked up towards the lighthouse, but there was no sign of her.

Surely Elsie hasn't been stupid enough to go off with the others? thought Rorie. They had been over and over the plan, and she should have been in no doubt that she was supposed to remain behind. The changing tent, perhaps? Rorie picked up her backpack and went to take a look.

No Elsie.

Rorie quickly changed into her own slants and baggy shirt. She was about to tie the Leesa Simms cravat around her neck, then realised she had better wait – she had to look for Elsie right away, and could hardly go prowling around like Dr Jekyll turning into Mr Hyde. She stuffed it back in her backpack and went in search. Now the pier was almost empty. To her left, the beach was filling up with holiday-makers. Surely Elsie wasn't so daft as to have gone off to play in the sand? A small girl momentarily caught Rorie's eye, but then turned around; it wasn't Elsie.

To the right of the pier was the yacht marina; row upon row of pleasure boats gleaming in the sunlight.

Suddenly Rorie caught sight of a small figure on the deck of a medium-sized sailing boat, waving both arms vigorously; within seconds she realised it was Elsie, wearing her funky wig.

'What the heck…?' Rorie ran towards the sailboat, her head jangling with questions. Who did they know with a sailboat in Cornwall? She could think of nobody. What on earth was Elsie up to?

Rorie slowed her pace slightly, not wanting to make herself conspicuous, although she was alarmed to see that Elsie, wig askew, appeared to be loosening the ropes the boat was moored with. Even more incredibly, she could hear the *gug gug gug* of its engine.

Rorie ran down the steps and along the jetty. 'Who are you with?' she called out as soon as she was close enough.

'No one!' replied Elsie as the boat began to drift away from the jetty, the ropes now completely freed. 'Come on, quick!'

Rorie glanced all around, then hissed, 'Are you crazy? Get out of there, this is nuts!' She reached for one of the ropes, but the boat veered away.

'Oops!' said Elsie, as the boat lurched sideways, sending its rear end rightwards, dangerously close to the neighbouring yacht. She attempted to straighten her wig. 'I think you steer it with this stick,' she said, grabbing hold of the tiller and wrenching it to the right. The boat swung even further, nudging against the other boat.

'No, no, you have to turn it the *other* way!' cried Rorie, remembering a rowing boat outing from the previous summer. She leapt aboard and grabbed the tiller, turning it to the left. The boat straightened out, but it was now some way away from the jetty. Rorie concentrated on keeping it steady so that it didn't crash into something, while she tried to figure out what on earth to do next.

'We are *not* getting away by stolen boat!' she hissed between gritted teeth. She peered at the assortment of dials, none of which made any sense to her. 'How do I reverse this thing?'

'We're not going back!' insisted Elsie, pushing on a control that made the boat surge forward with alarming speed; only a quick tug on the tiller from Rorie prevented it from crashing into the hull of another yacht.

'Elsie, *stop this*,' pleaded Rorie, tossing her head in an attempt to move the lock of hair that the wind had blown in her face.

'But how else are we going to get to New York?'

'Do *what*?!'

'You said Mum and Dad were in New York,' said Elsie. 'An' we have to get them back, right?'

'I never...' Rorie trailed off, dumbstruck. The workings of her little sister's mind never ceased to amaze her. She didn't know where to begin to explain all the things that were wrong with this crackpot plan, and she wasn't even going to try. All she could think of right now was how to avoid an accident – and avoid getting into trouble for attempting to steal a boat.

Now the boat was well away from the jetty, but there were more hazards ahead. Moored yachts loomed up on all sides: navigating their way in any direction would require knowledge and skills they didn't have. Rorie began to panic, and silently cursed her little sister for getting them into such a mess. She was also beginning to feel horribly conspicuous – especially as they seemed to have attracted the attention of a man on the pier, who was now heading towards them at a rapid pace.

'Look, I don't even know how to control this thing!' she told Elsie, her voice trembling with nerves.

Elsie blinked at her. She turned and dived into the cabin, returning almost instantly with a blue hat. She thrust it forward. 'Now you do!' she declared.

Chapter 15
New York

They were quickly advancing towards the adjacent row of boats and jetties, but Rorie had only just put the hat on, tucking in her hair as best she could, and it had yet to take effect. She turned the boat to the right – that much she was able to do. But she had not made the turn swiftly enough, and now the boat was heading straight for another vessel. What she really needed to do in order to straighten out and clear the marina was to put the boat in reverse, and as yet she had no idea how to do that. Meanwhile, the man on the pier was now coming down the steps – he would be upon them in no time.

Rorie gazed around. It looked as if the only manual control besides the tiller was the lever Elsie had used, apparently some sort of accelerator. She was just wondering what would happen if she pulled it in the opposite direction, when Elsie reached for it again. Rorie grabbed her wrist. 'Don't touch!' she growled. 'Get out of sight, down below. Someone's coming!'

Elsie, seeing the man, did as she was told.

'Hey,' Rorie called back to her, throwing her the precious backpack. 'Take this down. And get me any other clothes that are down there – quick!' She noticed with relief that her voice was deepening, as her first-ever masculine transformation took hold of her. There was the familiar queasiness as she felt her frame grow squarer, along with a new, almost indefinable sensation – a sort of manly confidence. She turned back to the controls. Ah! Now it was all coming together, like a blurry image slowly being brought into focus. This lever was the throttle; she needed to pull it. The boat, only seconds away from collision, pulled back.

Rorie's relief was momentary. 'The lines!' she exclaimed, seeing a rope dragging in the water behind them.

'What?' said Elsie, reappearing from the cabin with a thinfat jacket and a pair of flexishades. She threw them towards Rorie.

The man was getting closer.

'Never mind,' said Rorie in her new baritone voice.

'Get back down below before he sees you. And find yourself a life jacket!' At the same time she lunged to the side and grabbed hold of the stray rope – *the stern line*, said the sailor's jargon in her head. She pulled it swiftly onto the deck, then surveyed the other mooring lines that Elsie had untied from the dock, relieved to see that none of them were also dangling in the water.

Rorie hurriedly returned to the tiller and steadied the boat. Not daring to let go again, she reached down, grabbed the jacket and flexishades and quickly put them on, just as the man on the jetty appeared before her.

'Hey, Geoff, what's happening there?' the man called out. 'You got trouble?' The distance was just great enough – maybe ten metres – that Rorie's transformation, together with the partial disguise of the hat, jacket and shades, was apparently convincing enough.

Rorie looked at him, relieved to be addressed in this way, and now that she felt the transformation was complete – queasy though she was at the sight of a few dark curly hairs which poked out of her sleeves. 'Hey, Bill,' she replied deeply, with as much manly confidence as she could muster. 'No biggie. Damn stern line went over the side, thought it was going to wrap itself around the prop. All set now.'

Bill gave a sympathetic wince, hands on hips. 'Happened to me once. Can't be too careful.' He peered curiously along the length of the boat. 'You got enough help there?'

'Oh yeah. Mike's just gone down below to check the hatches and seacocks are tight,' said Rorie-as-Geoff, the boating jargon tripping effortlessly off her tongue. 'Well, catch you later,' she added, signing off with a macho flat-palmed gesture.

Bill remained on the jetty in his Superman pose, watching intently. This made Rorie more nervous than ever, and masculine sweat began to trickle down the sides of her lengthened, more angular face. She concentrated on the job at hand. Skilfully handling the throttle and the tiller, she guided the boat along the lane between the moored vessels.

'Hey, Geoff!' called Bill.

Oh no, now what? thought Rorie, panic rising in her stomach. 'Er, yeah?' she croaked.

Bill pointed. 'Don't forget your fenders.'

Embarrassed, Rorie managed to give Bill the thumbs up, as if to say, 'Sure, Bill, everything's cool,' – although the 'Geoff' part of her was painfully aware that a seasoned sailor would never leave it so long before pulling up the sausage-shaped bumpers that were only supposed to be hung over the side when the boat was moored.

But Bill, thankfully, seemed unconcerned and soon they were off, chugging steadily out of the marina.

Rorie took a deep breath of the salty air, not daring to look back. *Relax*, she told herself. *One thing at a time.* She *was* Geoff now – at least for as long as it took to get out of this whole mess with the boat. And to do that, Rorie-as-Geoff knew it was time to set sail. There was a good steady breeze blowing, and experience told her that this would get them away faster than the rather shrimpish engine ever could.

But even as the seafaring confidence took over, another, far greater worry was expanding like an angry red balloon in Rorie's mind: they were in deeper trouble than ever.

Elsie's head popped up from the cabin; she had removed the wig. 'Is the coast clear?' she asked gaily.

The red balloon burst. 'I've damn well had it with you!' Rorie yelled into the wind, unable to prevent a little Geoff-speak from creeping in. 'Why did I even *tell* you what I was planning to do? I should have just left you behind in la-la fashion-land where you belong!'

'But—'

'No! Don't try to justify yourself to me!' Rorie snapped, as she pulled in the fenders. 'I never said *anything* about stealing a boat!'

'Hey, *you* stole Aunt Irmine's jacket and car when we were escaping from Poker Bute Hall!' retorted Elsie.

'That was different!' shrieked Rorie. 'Look, just hold this *still*, do you hear?' she instructed, wrapping Elsie's hand around the tiller. She fastened Elsie's life jacket, then began pulling off the mainsail cover. 'It's not the same thing at all,' she went on, unashamedly enjoying the extra fierceness Geoff's tones lent to her voice. 'I had a strategy! Besides, that was only joy-riding, not stealing – well, with the car, at least.'

'But not the jacket.'

'Oh, *right*,' said Rorie sarcastically. 'I mean, jacket, ten-metre sailing boat – what's the difference, right?'

Ignoring this, Elsie said brightly, 'Hey, are you putting up the sail?'

'It does not mean what you think it means,' replied Rorie icily. 'It's just until…hold *steady*, for God's sake! Push the tiller to port…I mean left, I mean *that way*,' she yelled, waving her arm. 'So we move *away* from the land…that's it…it's very rocky around here, you've got to be careful. Look at that indicator there,' she said, pointing. 'What does it say?'

'Nineteen,' said Elsie.

Rorie pulled her hat down firmly around her ears and began untying the sail. 'OK, that's the depth of the water; gets any less than seven, you let me know right away, understand?'

'Okey-doke!' sang Elsie, still too blissfully excited about her big adventure to let small inconveniences like guilt or Rorie's anger get in the way.

'How the heck did you get this thing started, anyway?' demanded Rorie, slapping the ties down onto the deck.

'I saw the Geoff guy park the boat an' go in that bar place with his big dog, so I followed him. He was standing at the bar an' the dog was wagging its tail, *whack, whack*, against his trousers so he din't notice when I got the remote from his pocket.'

'And nobody else saw?'

'There was a bunch of people but they couldn'ta seen 'cause they were talking too loud.'

Rorie took this to mean the others were too absorbed in their conversation to notice anything. Well, at least that might buy them some time. The real Geoff probably wouldn't notice the missing remote any time soon – assuming he was finished sailing for the day. But this felt like small consolation to Rorie.

'And what in hell's name do you think's going to happen now, huh?'

'We sail to New York,' said Elsie simply. 'Hey, there it goes, whee!' she added, watching the mainsail as Rorie hoisted it up.

'Elsie,' said Rorie, pausing to give her sister a withering look. 'Do you have *any* idea how far away New York is?'

'You can get there in four hours,' said Elsie. 'I remember Dad told me that once.'

'By *plane*, Elsie!' cried Rorie. 'You can't just get in a little boat like this and sail across the Atlantic Ocean – well, you could, but only if you were trained up and had several days' worth of supplies... Elsie, it's really *dangerous*. We'd never survive!'

Elsie stared at her blankly. 'We could fish?'

Rorie stared back at her, open-mouthed. 'Look, I never said Mum and Dad were in New York, anyway.'

'Well, where else –' Elsie fell silent; something had caught her eye. 'What are those people doing?' she asked, pointing back towards the marina.

Rorie turned round. Two jet skis, like waterborne motorbikes, were advancing at an alarming rate and heading straight for them.

Chapter 16
Revenge of the Perfects

She stared at the approaching jet skis. The Rorie part of her brain said, *Oh no! Nolita's set the police on us,* while the Geoff part of her brain said, *These guys are out of control; get well clear of them!*

Having hoisted the sail, she hauled in the mainsheet, the rope which tightened it up, and soon she felt the boat speed up as it caught the wind. All the time she kept her sights on the jet skis: they were still heading directly for them.

Clutching onto her hat, Rorie jumped into the cockpit and switched off the motor, then dived for the tiller. 'Out of the way!' she demanded, elbowing Elsie aside. 'And keep down!'

'Are they chasing us?' yelled Elsie, as she threw herself down onto the seat and clung to the nearest winch.

'How do I know?' Rorie yelled back. 'I mean yes, *probably*.' She steered the boat slightly to port, and now the sail began to catch the wind beautifully. At last the boat tilted slightly and they felt themselves being carried along by the breeze.

But as Rorie glanced back, she could see their speed was no contest for the jet skis, which bounced noisily ever closer, vast white sprays spilling out behind them.

Now that the jet skis lined up alongside each other, Rorie could see that one of the riders had flowing white-blonde hair. 'No. It can't be...' she whispered.

Suddenly the blonde one shot forward, aiming directly at the hull of the boat. Rorie had no choice but to pull on the tiller, forcing the boat towards land. Then, at the last moment, the jet skier veered away. But seconds later, just as Rorie was correcting the boat's course, the other jet ski did exactly the same thing.

Rorie steadied the tiller, but now every part of her body was shaking. 'It's them!' she shouted to Elsie. 'Did you see? That was Nikki Deeds!'

Elsie, kneeling on her seat, peered over the side. 'And the other one was Leesa Simms.'

'How the hell did they find us?' said Rorie. As she watched the jet skis race on ahead, she knew this wasn't the last they would see of them. 'Grab the tiller again!' she shouted to Elsie. 'Hold it steady. I'm going to hoist the jib.'

'You're gonna what?'

'Never mind!'

Rorie bounced back and forth from side to side, fingers trembling as she untied a rope from a cleat on one side, then wrapped another one round the winch Elsie had been clinging to. As she pulled on this rope, the boat's second sail in front of the mast began to unfurl. Meanwhile, the jet skis were coming full circle, readying themselves for the next onslaught.

With the jib fully unfurled and filling with wind, Rorie returned to the tiller; as she did so, the boat heeled over even further to the left, throwing Elsie sideways. 'Aargh!' she cried, her legs waggling aloft like an overturned beetle. 'We're gonna tip over!'

'No, we're not; it's supposed to do that,' replied Rorie, pulling the peak of her sailing cap down securely. She was glad to note that their speed was now picking up considerably. 'Look, maybe you'd better get down below.'

'But—'

'Just do as I say!'

Elsie did as she was told.

Now the jet skis were returning. There were rocks jutting out up ahead, and Rorie felt a sickly, fiery chill as she realised what the two Perfects were trying to do: force her to crash into the rocks.

Again they pounded towards the boat. This time they actually bumped into the hull, knocking the boat into a dangerous tilt. Rorie slammed the tiller to the right, and just as the 'Geoff' part of her brain knew it would, this turned the boat further into the direction of the wind, which slackened the sails and pulled the boat upright again.

But it meant she was heading straight for the rocks.

With the boat now steady, and with the jet skis forming a wide arc, ready for the next attack, Rorie steered the boat back to catch the wind so that it headed away from the rocks. The Rorie thoughts and the Geoff thoughts were careering around in her head, trying to fit themselves around each other...

Rorie: *Aunt Irmine has sent them, acting on behalf of Uncle Harris. He wants you dead so that he can inherit everything from Great-Grandma. But you have one trick up your sleeve; they don't know that with this hat and jacket you are an experienced sailor...*

Geoff: *You can handle this; think of the toughest*

race and the most turbulent conditions you've sailed in. To get out of this, you will need to cause a very different kind of accident from the one they are expecting. Think of surprise tactics...

'Roreee!' cried Elsie from the cabin entrance.

'It's all right,' she called out.

'No, it isn't!' yelled Elsie, clutching a large water bottle. 'I can't stay down there, it's making me feel sick!'

'Well, come up then.'

Here came the jet skis again; Rorie-as-Geoff braced herself and shouted, 'Watch out!' to Elsie.

Slam slam slam they went over the water, and then they were upon them, *thud*. Then another thud, and another, and another. Rorie and Elsie both fell over. Now that the rocky outcrop was so close, the Perfects were actually *nudging* the boat towards the rocks. Rorie scrambled to her feet and lunged for the tiller. Elsie grabbed the water bottle and threw it over the side, hitting Nikki Deeds on the knee and throwing her briefly off kilter.

Rorie seized the moment; she clasped Elsie's hands around the tiller again. 'When I say, you turn it *that* way, OK?'

Not waiting for a response, she darted back onto

the roof of the cabin. The black, glistening rocks were looming ever closer: Rorie could even feel the spray from the waves that were crashing against them. Gritting her teeth, she forced herself to follow the instructions in her head and tightened the rope attached to the front sail.

'Rorie! It's gone down to five!' yelled Elsie.

'What has?'

'That number thingy…you told me to tell you if it went less than seven.'

'Yes, yes, all right,' replied Rorie, sounding increasingly shrill. She couldn't worry about running aground now. She checked on the jet skis – they were pounding towards them again, faster than ever. 'And…now!' she called to Elsie. '*That* way!'

Elsie yanked on the tiller; Rorie scrambled across the boat, grabbed the rope on the other side and pulled hard, upon which the jib switched sides and the boat began to turn inward, side-on to the rocks. Above her head the mainsail also caught the wind on the other side as the boom swung from right to left. The boat rocked like a cradle, now sucked in, now spat out by the tide against the rocks. Then, all of a sudden, both sails plumped out, pulling them clear of the rocks at the very last moment.

Crash! The Perfects, having accelerated hard for a good thump against the boat, were not prepared for it to turn about so abruptly. They banked hard but lost control. Both girls leapt from their vehicles, which smashed into the rocks.

Chapter 17
Catrina Cut-Throat

'How did they find us?' asked Elsie, once they were well out to sea, away from rocks, land and Perfects.

With the autohelm guiding the boat, Rorie lay stretched out on the bench, staring up at the sky. Still in a state of shock, she was trying to process everything that had happened. 'I don't know,' she said vaguely. 'Hey, get me a beer, will you?'

'What!'

'Oh, hang on. That was Geoff talking there!' Rorie pulled the hat off and threw it into the cabin. 'I'm fed up with being him.'

'But you've got a boat to sail!'

'All right, it's under control!' said Rorie irritably, shaking out her hair. 'Just let me be *me* for a while, OK? Oh, my hands are *killing* me!' Red welts and blisters had bubbled up all over her palms. But Rorie watched with satisfaction as the coarse hairs on her wrists began to recede, and her fingers became slender once more. 'You know what?'

'What?'

'I bet Aunt Irmine's had those girls spying on us all along,' said Rorie, her voice returning to normal. 'But with all those security people of Nolita's, they couldn't get at us before now. The only time I've been anywhere alone was when I went to see Inspector Dixon – but I was without you, and they wanted both of us.'

'I guess so,' said Elsie.

Rorie sighed. 'Wow. I knew they were evil, but I never thought they'd actually try to *kill* us...'

'D'you fink they've drownded?' asked Elsie.

'No,' said Rorie. 'Nikki Deeds drown, are you kidding? I'll bet she swims like a killer whale...more's the pity.'

For a moment, only the sound of the sea, the gulls and the slapping of rope against mast filled the air, as the two of them contemplated their narrow escape. Rorie found her thoughts wandering to Nolita, and she tried to picture what she was doing at that moment. By now she would have realised they were missing, and the thought made Rorie feel queasy...

'Hey, I gotta tell you something!' said Elsie suddenly, grabbing Rorie's arm. '*Guess what.*'

Rorie propped herself up on her elbows. 'What?'

'There's a *whole house* on this boat,' said Elsie, eyes round with excitement. 'It's downstairs. There's bedrooms, an' a loo, an' a whole *kitchen*!'

'I know. So?'

'*So*...we can live in it till we get to New York!'

Rorie slumped back down, speechless. She gazed at a seagull as it circled overhead. What on earth was she to do now? She was determined to find Mum and Dad, that much she knew. But how? Her mind was a blank. They couldn't possibly sail to New York – though for all she knew their parents might be there...or in Shanghai, or Kuala Lumpur...

It was mind-boggling.

Once again she remembered the big, beautiful butterfly she had dreamt of, and wondered, *What would Mum and Dad do?* And soon the words of one of Dad's problem-solving mantras entered her head: *Start with what you know.*

Well, we're probably officially 'missing' at this point, thought Rorie; that ought to help. Because as long as no one knew where they were, they were free to do their own detective work. And Rorie was accumulating disguises all the time – she had five of them now. Though there was still the matter of Elsie...plus it was probably only a matter of time before a police helicopter would be circling above them...

'Well?' prompted Elsie, eagerly awaiting a response.

Rorie couldn't face another battle right now. Trying to explain everything that was wrong with Elsie's idea felt like trying to untangle a mass of knotted ropes. So she resorted to fiction – a bedtime story for her little sister. 'All right,' she said at last. 'We sail to New York.'

'Ahoy there!' cried Elsie, as she wobbled in her bare feet, clinging to the mast.

Rorie watched her from the tiller and smiled. Somehow her irritation towards Elsie had subsided, probably because she felt so elated herself. She was exhilarated by the vast, empty grey-green water all around her, the vast, empty sky above; the sense that here was a blank slate, a fresh start. The choices of where to go from here were limitless. 'There's no land or ships in sight, Elsie,' she pointed out. 'You're only supposed to say "ahoy there" to landlubbers or other sailors.'

'I don't care, I like saying it. Anyway, I'm not Elsie,

I'm…Catrina Cut-Throat, the most dangerous pirate in all of the Caribbean Sea!'

'Oh, OK,' said Rorie, not wanting to spoil things by mentioning the fact that they were actually in the Celtic Sea, just a few kilometres west of the Cornwall coast. The wind had eased, and the sea was quite calm. The boat was sailing gently in a north-westerly direction, only slightly tilting. Pretty soon they would have to change direction…but not just yet. 'Who am I then?' she asked Elsie, humouring her.

'Arr, matey! You be the evil captain.' Elsie retrieved the hat and jumped down into the cockpit. 'Come on, put it on!'

'No!' said Rorie, leaning away. 'I'm not putting that thing on again until I have to.'

'Spoilsport,' complained Elsie. 'You're way uglier with it on. It would be so much better for the game.'

'Exactly why I don't want to put it on,' said Rorie. 'But don't wave it about like that; put it down below where it's safe. We mustn't lose it!'

'Avast ye! I'll slice ye wi' me cutlets!' growled Elsie, attacking an imaginary assailant as she emerged from the cabin.

'You mean *cutlass*,' corrected Rorie. The mention of cutlets, however, made her realise she hadn't eaten since that morning, which seemed a whole lifetime away now. For some reason, though, she wasn't hungry; she was still buzzing from all the excitement of the escape. Now, an even more thrilling realisation dawned on her. 'Elsie?' she said.

'Not Elsie. Catrina!'

'OK, *Catrina*. Have you noticed something?'

'Yeah! We're real live pirates!'

'OK, we're pirates,' said Rorie impatiently. 'But, Elsie, look: we've been out here for nearly an hour now, and no one's coming after us.'

Elsie shrugged. 'Yeah, well, we 'scaped from the Perfects, din't we?'

'I'm not talking about them, I'm talking about the police,' said Rorie. 'They've got satellite tracking, they'd be able to get a helicopter after us, easy...but they haven't, have they?'

Elsie surveyed the skies, squinting. 'Don't look like it.'

Rorie gazed all around. 'It's weird. You'd think Nolita would send them after us, wouldn't you?'

Elsie shrugged. 'Maybe she thinks we'll come back when we want to.'

'Don't be daft! She...' Rorie paused. 'Hang on. Maybe she doesn't want us back!' Suddenly, this rang true to her. 'Maybe she's decided we're too much trouble…or *I* am, after snooping through her files. In which case she really must have something to hide, and we're better off away from her.'

Elsie frowned and chewed her lip.

'*But*,' said Rorie, 'there's also the small matter of this stolen boat. It seems this Geoff guy hasn't noticed that his boat's gone yet.'

'Prob'ly he went home,' said Elsie.

'I guess so,' said Rorie. 'In which case we've got at least until tomorrow, and possibly longer, before he finds out and reports it.'

This led Rorie back to the question she'd been avoiding: what to do next? Returning the boat to its mooring in St Ives seemed far too risky now, even in her 'Geoff' guise. She supposed they could find their way to some other place along the coast…somewhere secluded. But how on earth would she do that?

Elsie interrupted her thoughts. 'So by the time the Geoff guy finds his boat missing, we'll be well on our way to New York! How long's it gonna take to get there?'

'Look, Elsie, about that –'

'What?'

'The problem is…'

'We *have* to go!' exclaimed Elsie. 'How else are we going to find Mum and Dad? Rorie, you promised!'

'I just said that to keep you quiet,' said Rorie. 'We *can't* go to New York – it's five and a half thousand kilometres away!'

'OOOWWOOWOO!' howled Elsie.

'Look, I never said they were there!' protested Rorie. 'You just got it into your head that they were...and in any case we would *die*, Elsie. We'd die!' Her voice grew louder with frustration.

Elsie went on howling.

Rorie tried a different approach. 'Look,' she said, putting an arm around her sister. 'Let's see what's down below to eat – or at least make some tea or something – and talk this over. OK?'

The mention of food seemed to calm Elsie a little. 'OK.'

Once Elsie had settled down, Rorie found she was reluctant to discuss the New York issue further and get her upset all over again. Why did she need a silly seven-year-old's permission anyway? She was the captain, wasn't she? She was in charge. Besides, Elsie was bound to get tired sometime over the next few hours. Rorie decided she would just have to try and change direction single-handedly while Elsie slept.

It had seemed like a good plan, until Mother Nature intervened.

They hadn't long finished their late, late lunch – there had been a vacuum-pack of corned beef and half a packet of crackers in among the several six-packs of beer – when Rorie began to notice foamy white crests forming on the waves. 'Sea's getting rougher,' she remarked.

'Oo-arr!' cried Elsie, back on her pirate kick. 'Look out! There's a storm a-brewin'!'

Rorie went down to the cabin and checked the weather satellite; there was indeed a storm developing to the southeast of them – exactly the direction she had intended to turn towards. She felt stupid. All this time she had been blithely sailing along, not bothering to wear the skipper's hat for guidance, not thinking that it was necessary because everything seemed to be going so well. She felt *more* than stupid: she felt afraid. They were still much nearer to Cornwall than to Ireland or Wales, yet to turn back would be to ride directly into the storm. They were much too far from anywhere for comfort. It was time for Rorie to transform back into a proper captain; one who knew what he was doing. She reached for Geoff's hat.

'Hey, that's better!' said Elsie, when Rorie came

back up on deck, complete with hat, thinfat jacket, and very different face. 'Now you can join in the game and be Captain Hook!'

'No, damn it!' said Rorie-as-Geoff (Geoff did seem to say 'damn' a lot). 'Get down from there; there really is a storm coming. And you're going to get cold and wet – go down and find yourself a warm jacket. It'll be too big for you, but it'll have to do.'

Elsie went below.

'And put your...' Rorie trailed off. No point in telling Elsie to put her shoes on – they were silver wedge sandals. Elsie was better off barefoot, in true pirate style, though her feet were going to freeze. 'Never mind,' Rorie sighed.

The sky was turning a leaden grey; just a thin streak of light now showed on the horizon, the last of the clear sky receding into the distance. *Clank, clank!* went the rigging on the mast as the wind gathered. Rorie instinctively lunged back as she felt the boat heel over alarmingly.

She heard a loud *clunk!* from down below, as Elsie fell against the side. 'Ow!'

'It's OK,' called Rorie, as she hurriedly pulled in the mainsail. The boat levelled out somewhat, and Elsie came back out on deck.

But before long the waves were swelling and plummeting so much that Rorie began to feel very nervous. Elsie, seated securely in the cockpit and clinging tightly to the nearest winch, just whooped and yelped with delight. 'Wheee! It's like at the fair!' she cried, shrieking with laughter every time she got sprayed with saltwater. Rorie's heart was pounding as she concentrated all her energy on keeping everything under control. Even with the reduced sail they were pulling along at a fair clip now, and it took some considerable effort to keep the sails angled in the increasingly blustery winds.

Hulking great clouds were looming overhead and gigantic raindrops pelted down angrily. *Clang clang clang!* went the lines against the mast, with increasing urgency, as if sounding an alarm. The sea moaned and gushed as it sent its briny spray up to mingle with the rain again, and again, and again. Great heaving mounds of foamy iron-grey sea sent the boat tilting and heaving. Elsie was silent now; this was definitely not like the fair any more. Her face gleamed as white as glistening bone, and she began to whimper. 'Oh Rorie, I'm think I'm going to—', but she didn't finish her sentence. Her whole frame convulsed, and she quickly yanked herself up by the guardrail and vomited over the side.

Rorie was aware of a mild sense of relief that Elsie had managed to throw up into the sea – and also that she would at least now shut up – but this did little to quell her overriding sense of sheer, blinding terror. For here she was, once again, out in a storm, with little to protect her. What if she were struck by lightning again? What if Elsie were struck? They might not be lucky enough to survive this time.

For the longest two hours of her life, Rorie braved it out at the tiller in a welter of anxiety and sodden concentration, her face locked in a wet, determined grimace, her hands almost numb from gripping so hard.

Evening fell. Every now and then Elsie would throw up again. Finally, weakened and exhausted, she just managed to put on the boat's lights as Rorie had instructed, before disappearing into the cabin.

Still the storm raged. Rorie didn't think it was possible for things to get any worse than they already were.

Then, they did.

Chapter 18
Bareheaded Blues

A peaked cotton cap is not exactly the right sort of headgear to wear in a storm. Especially if you are a twelve-year-old girl attempting to sail a ten-metre vessel, single-handedly, with no previous experience. Even allowing for the chameleon factor, it was a tall order.

Rorie did her utmost to keep Geoff's hat from flying off, jamming it down over her ears regularly, but eventually the inevitable happened. A huge gust of wind whipped it up, and in an instant it was gone. *Well, thank God I have the jacket*, thought Rorie. But then, to her horror, she began to feel the unmistakable sensation that she was shrinking, transforming back into her normal self. She looked at her hands: yes, the fingers were becoming paler, smaller; the coarse dark hairs at the wrist receding... She felt inside the collar of the jacket, and pulled out a plastic tag with a label attached – the jacket was brand-new, unworn. The flexishades were no good…even if they had any effect, she wouldn't be able to see anything. Only the hat had been of any use, and that was gone. With it went all of Geoff's seafaring knowledge. All Rorie was left with was what she had already learnt.

Still she struggled on, trying to ignore the feeling of panic that kept threatening to overwhelm her. *Things aren't all that bad*, she resolutely told herself, as she tugged on the mainsheet, the rope which held the mainsail in place, desperately trying keep the boat from heeling too far. *You've learnt a lot from what you've done already. And the storm* will *end…*

Then the mainsheet snapped.

This sent the sail out of control, its boom nearly knocking Rorie out. She grabbed it and clung on – she hadn't a clue what else to do. The broken mainsheet whipped around like crazy, and Rorie began to sob, silent in the wind as she yanked it out of the cleat and tossed it into the sea.

We're going to die, was all she could think now. She felt herself being swallowed up by blackness…

No! She would *not* let that happen. Some kind of fire flared up inside her, freshly stoked; it filled her with a new energy. *Stabilise the sail*, it said – *there has to be a way… Find a way, now!*

The mooring line, that was it! Rorie set the autohelm, then unwound the nearest mooring line with trembling, half-frozen hands. Still sobbing and drenched with rain, she tried rigging it as a new mainsheet. She knew she was clutching at straws; all she had was the memory of Geoff's knowledge, and this was a new situation…yet the line pulled through the blocks easily, and to her amazement she soon had the sail back under control. She heaved a massive sigh of relief and sat back down by the helm, still pulling hard on the mainsheet against the force of the wind.

The storm raged on. In spite of her small triumph, Rorie began to despair. Right now, she wished she were just about anywhere other than here – even Poker Bute Hall. Anywhere dry and safe. For the umpteenth time she cursed her little sister and her stupid, harebrained idea of stealing a boat and sailing to New York. Rorie could still hardly believe how she'd let this happen. So much for rescuing Mum and Dad – they themselves were going to need rescuing. With a heavy heart, Rorie resolved to send out a distress signal. She went down below.

But looking at the array of computer and radio

equipment, she was truly stumped. She took several deep breaths in an effort to calm herself; she *would* figure it out. She decided first to find out where they were: 59 kilometres northwest of St Ives, or approximately 9 hours' travelling time. Was that all? It felt as if they had gone so much further! Her heart sank as she realised it was still by far the nearest port – they would have to return there. And any ideas she'd had about coming ashore somewhere obscure soon dissolved when she saw how rocky the whole coastline was; it was far too risky to try anything fancy. But then a glimmer of hope: checking the weather forecast, she saw that the storm was decreasing. They were over the worst of it. If she could just keep going a little longer, perhaps she wouldn't have to send out a distress signal after all.

Next, Rorie looked in on Elsie. Somehow she was actually sleeping through the turmoil like the lullaby baby in the treetops, swaddled in twisted bedding. Well, she was certainly being rocked. Rorie was deeply envious. Elsie could just sleep away, while her sister sorted everything out. But who was there to help Rorie? No one. How wonderful it would be right now to be like Nolita, and have someone like Misty to call on whenever the going got rough. A quick reboot, and she would be able to see right away just what she needed to do.

Oh well. Rorie sighed, and forced herself to go back out on deck.

Ah, yes! The torrent was easing. They *would* survive; she was sure of it now. She thanked the heavens that there had been no lightning.

Great walls of water had reduced to mere hillocks; soon hillocks eased into a field of rippling tufts. Rorie took advantage of the weakened wind to turn the boat around. Even though she had to do it all by herself, relying solely on what she could remember from last time, she was unfazed; nothing could be as bad now as what she had been through. She moved about as if in a dream, turning the boat, then swinging the mainsail from right to left. Now that they were on course for St Ives, she set the autohelm. She didn't know how they'd get ashore undetected, but she couldn't worry about that now. Finally, she got a thinfat quilt from the cabin and settled down on deck with it wrapped around her, so she could keep watch through the night. But her good intentions amounted to nothing: within minutes she was fast asleep.

Rorie woke with a start, panic-stricken. She should

never have fallen asleep! Still groggy and confused, she couldn't work out why everything was grey. There was no horizon; just flat pale grey in every direction. All that was visible was the boat itself, and the calm water immediately below. Everything else was blank. Even the bow of the boat disappeared into nothingness. Rorie checked her watch – it was 5.30 am. Gradually, she became aware of a strange beeping from down below. Fully awake now, she went down into the cabin to investigate.

Beep beep beep beep... The noise was coming from the global positioning screen. Instead of displaying details of their location, there were the words:

SATELLITE COMMUNICATION FAILURE.
REVERSE COURSE TO RESUME GUIDANCE.

'Whass that noise?' came Elsie's voice from behind her.

Rorie tried to speak, but fear had dried out her mouth. She took a swig of water, and said, 'Um, there's some problem with this piece of equipment.'

Elsie peered at the screen, but the long words confused her. 'Whass it say?'

'Just that it's – um – it's telling us to turn around.'

'But we can't!' cried Elsie.

For once Rorie had to agree with her. She had been asleep for about six hours, and they had been on course for St Ives all that time. 'I know,' she said. 'By my reckoning, we ought to reach the shore in about three hours. It would be crazy to turn around now. If we just keep going, maybe the fog will clear.'

'The fog?'

'Oh, uh, yeah. There's this fog out there like you wouldn't believe.'

'Is that why it's telling us to turn around?'

'Hmm…well, I'm no expert, but surely the fog shouldn't make any difference? Mind you, I've never seen fog like this in my life. It's so thick you could practically slice it like cheese.'

'Really?' Elsie peered out of the cabin, then went up on deck to get a better look.

Rorie tried consulting the other instruments. But she could get no radio signal – only the good old-fashioned compass could be relied on.

That was when she got a nasty shock: the compass was pointing *west*.

Rorie suppressed a little gasp. West? They were supposed to be heading southeast! What on earth had happened?

'What's the matter?' asked Elsie, reappearing on the steps.

'What? Oh, nothing. Just checking, um, the direction...' Rorie tapped the compass, to see if it was stuck; it didn't waver. 'Erm, I...just have to nip up on deck for a moment, Else, OK? Then I'll, uh, fix some breakfast.'

It was when Rorie checked the autohelm that she finally realised what had happened. It had two settings: one to stay on course, and the other to follow the wind. Last night, exhausted, she had mistakenly set it to the latter. Then the boat had gradually rotated while she slept, following the wind. When the wind had changed, she had no idea – she couldn't begin to calculate where they might be right now. All she knew for sure was that they were now heading further and further out into the Atlantic Ocean.

Chapter 19
Strange Statue

'But you said we'd be crazy to change direction now!' protested Elsie.

'We're not changing direction exactly,' replied Rorie. 'Just...adjusting it a little. You have to do that once in a while. Now, do as I tell you.'

'But I'm *hungry*.'

'You'll get some breakfast after this. Now come on, lean over the side there.'

Rorie turned the helm and the boat began to rotate, but she found this made her feel ill. Not having a horizon to look at disoriented her and made her feel nauseous. 'OK, hang on,' she said, taking some deep breaths. *Perhaps we'd better do this in stages*, she thought. The feeling was just too weird. She set the autohelm, making sure it was set to stay on course this time; they were now heading north. 'All right. Breakfast.'

'Breakfast' consisted of water and crackers. Elsie also found a chocolate bar, which she ate greedily, her nose pressed against the window. 'Hey, I think the fog's going now.'

'It is?' Rorie hurried up onto the deck. 'You're right. You can see the whole of the front of the boat now.'

Elsie followed her up. 'Oh yeah!'

'Oh, Elsie, we're gonna be all right!' cried Rorie, peering in every direction for more signs. 'Look!' she said, as she gazed out at what she could see of the water. 'It's actually *lifting up*...see?'

'It's spooky,' remarked Elsie gleefully, already miraculously cured of her anxiety attack. 'Hey, let's play ghost ships!'

'Not now,' said Rorie. 'Listen: the GPS is still beeping... Oh, *please* let it start working again! As long as we can tell where we are, we'll be all right.'

'I wish the beeping would stop,' said Elsie. 'It's so annoying!'

Rorie stared ahead intently, trying to work out whether the fog really was clearing for good, or whether they had just happened upon a thin patch. She gazed into the grey-fading-to-whiteness, waiting for the horizon to appear.

The whiteness grew whiter.

The whiteness became a blue-tinged haze, and more and more water became visible. In the east there now appeared a softly glowing white ball in the sky.

'The sun!' cried Elsie. 'I can see the sun!'

Rorie turned around. 'Yes! Oh, *yes*...'

But the beeping continued: they still had no navigation system.

Then, when Rorie turned to face the bow once again, her jaw dropped. She couldn't believe her eyes.

'Hey, we're there!' cried Elsie. 'We're at New York!'

Rorie stood motionless as she took it all in: there was the Statue of Liberty, in all her glory; there were downtown Manhattan skyscrapers, dominated by the Freedom Tower...and the top of the Empire State Building was just visible. 'No, no, it can't be!' she gasped.

'What do you mean, it can't be? It is...just look!' shrieked Elsie. 'Hurray, we're here! We made it!'

'No, Elsie, this is *nuts*,' insisted Rorie. 'I must be dreaming!'

Elsie pinched her on the arm. 'See? You're *not*. It's real!'

'But it *can't* be...'

Elsie wasn't listening any more. 'Yay-hay, we're here! New York Citeeee!' she yelled, dancing around like a lunatic.

Meanwhile Rorie paced back and forth, every now and then gazing in disbelief at the vision ahead of them. 'It isn't possible,' she muttered, shaking her head. 'We've been travelling for...about fifteen hours. New York is...what? Five or six thousand kilometres from where we set out? We'd have had to be travelling at...' She paused as she called on her stressed-out, sleep-deprived brain for a rough calculation. '...At least three hundred kilometres an hour – no, *more*. It's impossible!'

The beeping carried on down below, a reminder that the global positioning still wasn't working even though the fog had almost cleared now, revealing a beautiful sunny day.

'...And we can't even check our location,' Rorie muttered on. 'But there's no way...I just don't understand...'

Elsie wasn't listening. '...*I – want – to* wake *up in the* city *that never* sleeps!' she sang, quoting a recent Paloma Vega rehash of some ancient song.

'Elsie, stop!' snapped Rorie, at last. 'This is not New York. It *can't* be.'

'But it is!' insisted Elsie. 'Just look at it!'

'Maybe it's...some other city that looks like it in, uh, Wales or somewhere,' suggested Rorie feebly.

Elsie blinked at her. 'What, there's some *other* place with a Statchoo Aliberty?'

Rorie shrugged. 'There might be...' *But an Empire State Building as well?* she thought. *A Freedom Tower?*

Meanwhile, New York City was advancing majestically towards them. Lady Liberty loomed in front of it all, curls of mist still shrouding her plinth while her golden torch glinted in the newly revealed sunlight. She was so ridiculously familiar that seeing her for the first time made Rorie want to cry and laugh at the same time. And, like most of the other celebrities Nolita had introduced her to, she was rather smaller than Rorie had expected.

'I fort she was bigger'n that,' remarked Elsie, gazing up at the statue.

'So did I... OK, maybe this isn't some other city,' said Rorie. 'But this is *really weird*, Elsie. You've got to understand just how weird it is! We can't have been going, like, three hundred and fifty kilometres an hour. Even at our fastest we were only doing maybe *seven* kilometres an hour. It's... Unless we've gone through some sort of time warp, or something...'

'What's a time warp?'

'It's...no, that doesn't happen in real life!'

'Well, I don't care how we got here,' announced Elsie firmly, folding her arms. 'We're *here*. That's what matters.'

'We're...' Rorie began, then trailed off. In a sense, Elsie was right. Who cared if it didn't make any sense how they had got there? What mattered was that they had found land. They were saved! They weren't going to die after all. 'All right. Look, I'm as relieved as you are,' said Rorie. 'But...hey, I just thought of something. The Leesa Simms cravat!'

Elsie wrinkled her nose. 'What about it?'

'That's it,' said Rorie, heading down into the cabin. 'I don't know why I didn't think of it before. She might know what to do with the global positioning, what with all her techie know-how! I should put on her cravat – *then* we can figure out where we are.'

Elsie sighed loudly, hands on hips. 'We're in *New York*...'

Rorie didn't answer; by now she was down below, fishing around in her backpack. She found the cravat and put it on, then braced herself for the transformation. *Ugh*, she thought, as she pictured

Leesa Simms in her head. Leesa, with her helmet of black hair, potato face and the personality of a prison warden. Rorie tried not to think about it, turning her attention instead to her desire to solve the mystery of where they were. She scrunched her eyes tight shut and waited.

It was an odious sensation. Not only did her clothing tighten so much that she had to loosen her waistband, but it made her face ache. Added to that was the strange sense of something alien entering her bloodstream. When she opened her eyes, she knew the transformation was complete – but everything was out of focus.

She let out a little yelp – unheard by Elsie, who was too busy singing, '*It's up to you, Noo York, Noooo Yoooork*.'

For a moment, Rorie was panic-stricken – until she realised what had happened. Leesa Simms was short-sighted, yet Rorie didn't have any glasses. Of course everything was out of focus! Sure enough, as she brought her hand closer to her face, the image crystallised before her.

Rorie-as-Leesa groped around for the chair and sat down, then squinted closely at the communications equipment. She checked its settings; the wireless connection...everything Leesa's brilliant technical mind could think of. 'There's nothing wrong with the system,' she concluded. 'Which leaves two possible explanations: atmospheric interference, and jamming.'

'*A-number-one! Queen of the hill! A-number—*' sang Elsie.

'Will you shut up!' snapped Rorie-as-Leesa.

Elsie shut up.

'We can eliminate the atmospheric theory, since we are no longer affected by fog...and in any case, that would only cause inaccuracies, not shut down the system altogether...'

Elsie just frowned.

'Which means the satellite signal has been deliberately jammed.'

'I don't know what you're talking about,' said Elsie.

'...Which *means* we're in danger, Elsie. We're not wanted here.'

Elsie looked shocked. 'But we're nice!'

'I'm not even going to dignify that with a response,' retorted Rorie pompously.

'Ugh! You sound just like Leesa Simms!' complained Elsie.

Rorie pulled off the cravat. 'Good point. What's more, I'm blind as a bat. I'm going to need my

eyes...probably some athletic skill as well, I reckon...'
She reached into her backpack and took out the Nikki
Deeds trainers. Her mind was racing, as the awfulness
of her dilemma began to hit home. Either sail away
and confront the dangers of the sea once again – not
to mention possible starvation – or go ashore, and risk
being attacked by whatever hostile people were here.
Not for a moment did she ever seriously contemplate
turning back.

Elsie watched as Rorie's appearance began to blend
straight from black-haired potato-face to lithe-limbed
blonde, with no Rorie in between.

'Wait here, OK?' said Rorie-as-Nikki, and she
stumbled up to the deck, her sight still a little blurry.
She clambered onto the roof of the cabin; she already
knew this was where the life raft was, having
contemplated using it in her most desperate moments.
The adrenaline was pumping through her veins. It
occurred to her that she could send out a smoke signal
as a decoy, then with any luck get away in the life raft
undetected. As she set about the task of unstrapping
the life raft canister a foghorn sounded, making her
jump. Looking up, the vision of a ferryboat came
gradually into focus, as Leesa's short-sightedness
receded. The boat was sailing from port to starboard,

about fifty metres away.

It was just as well Rorie did look up, because as she did, she caught sight of the Statue of Liberty.

And that was doing something very strange indeed.

Chapter 20
The Candyfloss Woman

Lady Liberty's arm was no longer holding her torch skywards: it was lowering.

'Elsie!' cried Rorie-as-Nikki, as she frantically studied the instructions for the life raft. 'Get up here, quick – and bring the backpack!'

Rorie threw the life raft overboard and tugged on the line to inflate it. As it began to balloon out, she cast her eye around for anything else she thought she should bring. *Ropes*, she thought. She opened one of the storage bins and found one, slinging it over her arm. She glanced nervously at the statue – Lady Liberty's arm had now lowered even further...and was pointing in their direction.

Elsie appeared. 'Oh Rorie, I'm scared!'

The life raft seemed to be fully inflated now, so Rorie grabbed the backpack from Elsie and made towards it. 'We have to abandon ship,' she explained hurriedly. 'I'll go first.' And with that, she leapt swiftly overboard with Nikki Deeds's characteristic grace and landed in the raft. Salt spray showered her as she quickly straightened out and reached up for Elsie. 'Jump!' she ordered. 'I'll catch you!'

Just as Elsie got airbound, a beam of light shot down from Lady Liberty's torch and hit the boat.

The explosion created a force that sent Elsie hurtling forwards like a rag doll. 'Elsie!' cried Rorie, as her sister landed so heavily in the life raft it almost capsized. Ears ringing, Rorie rowed frantically away from the flaming boat, the belching smoke and the shower of shrapnel. 'Elsie...*are you all right?*' she demanded urgently.

Elsie stirred slowly. 'I dunno...'

As Rorie rowed, she looked anxiously up at the ferryboat. She wasn't near enough to be able to read the passengers' faces, but she was suddenly chilled to the bone as she realised that the burst of sound she had heard immediately following the explosion had not been a ringing in her ears, but a rousing cheer: the passengers had been applauding the apparent vanquishing of an enemy. But what else could she do?

She rowed with all her might, heading towards the ferryboat.

'Else?'

'Yeah?' came the croaky response.

'Can you move? I need to know if you're hurt.'

Elsie slowly sat up. 'I fink I'm OK. What happened?'

'We were attacked by your beloved New York City. And there's something seriously weird going on here.' She gazed at the flaming boat. 'Well, at least I didn't need to send out that smoke signal.'

'Huh?'

'Listen, we're going to try to get ashore – but it's extremely risky. You have to obey me at all times, you understand? Or we could get ourselves killed. We can only hope that the flames and smoke coming from the boat right now provide cover while we stow away on that ferry.'

'How we gonna get up there?' asked Elsie, as they drew nearer.

Rorie gazed up nervously at the sheer side of the ferryboat. The back end, which was nearest, had an open deck, as did the front, while the middle section was covered. It was much bigger than it had seemed from a distance. 'Well…see that gate up there? There's some sort of doorknob-type things either side of it; if I can just get the rope secured around it, I could climb up...'

'What about me?'

'You'll be on my back.'

'*What?* You're kidding!'

Rorie shot Elsie a piercing look. 'I am deadly serious,' she said, pulling out the rope. 'Look, I can do it, OK? Because Nikki Deeds can do it; I know she can. You don't weigh anything, anyway...er...' She stalled as she wound the rope this way and that, trying to figure out how to knot it. She cursed the moment she'd lost Geoff's hat – *he* no doubt was an expert at this...

'You want some help there?' asked Elsie.

'You?'

'Yeah,' said Elsie. 'Cammy teached me. Friendship bracelets.' Elsie held up her wrist to show her the one she was wearing.

'Oh, Else, I don't think that's the right kind...'

'She showed me other knots too, 'cause I was really into it.' Elsie grabbed the rope. 'You need a slipknot, so it'll loop onto the thingy and tighten when you yank it,' she said, as she went about making the knot.

Rorie gazed at her, open-mouthed. 'Amazing. And

there I was thinking all you'd been learning about was dresses.'

'See? I do know useful stuff, too,' said Elsie, presenting Rorie with the finished knot.

'Thank you.' Rorie took the rope and hurled it up. It wasn't easy, with the life raft sloshing around all over the place. But after a couple of attempts, the rope caught. Rorie tugged to secure it, then zipped up the backpack and handed it to Elsie. 'OK, you'll have to wear this, and I'll wear you. Just hold on *tight*...that's really important, Elsie. Right, here goes.'

Rorie had to ease herself up gently, since there was no possibility of launching herself off the life raft. To start with it was very wet and tough going – especially with a seven-year-old clamped onto her. Even an exceptionally light seven-year-old like Elsie was a considerable burden, and Rorie had to use every ounce of her strength to haul herself up. By now her hands were so blistered they felt as if they were on fire. But she *had* to keep going – the life raft had drifted away...

About halfway up, it started to get a little easier, as Rorie gathered momentum, bouncing her way higher. At last she reached the guardrail...where she was greeted by a crowd of passengers, staring down at her.

They were mostly elderly, but looked much like any group of holiday-makers anywhere.

'Hello!' cried a little boy, waving as he bent over the rail. 'Hello!'

'Oh wow,' murmured Rorie. 'We've been rumbled.'

'Never mind,' whispered Elsie. 'They seem friendly.'

'Oh, *Else*...'

A round of applause greeted them as they came on board. *Funny*, thought Rorie: weren't these the same people she had heard cheering the destruction of their boat? Whose side were they on? Unless she had imagined it... All the same, she decided they had better pretend they had nothing to do with that boat, though she wasn't sure how likely it was that they would believe her.

All eyes were on them, watching expectantly for an explanation.

'Oh!' Rorie gasped, as she put Elsie down and struggled to get her breath back. 'That explosion...we were just out, you know mucking about in our dinghy...gone a bit far out, I guess! Yes, well, and then next thing we know there's this *pchhhooom!* and bits were falling...we got a puncture, see, and—'

'You were lucky,' said an old woman with unfeasibly yellow candyfloss hair.

'You need a nurse?' asked the tall, silver-haired man standing beside her.

Rorie hesitated. Her hands were screaming out with pain, but she decided it was safer not to have contact with anyone who might ask awkward questions. She stuffed her hands in her pockets. 'N-no, we're fine. You're OK, aren't you...uh?' she asked Elsie, thinking she would give her a fake name but at the last moment thinking better of it, in case Elsie didn't catch on.

'Yeah,' said Elsie.

'So you're not the TPs then?' asked another man.

'The what?'

'The TPs. The trespassers. From that boat,' explained the silver-haired man. He had mottled brown skin and an unnerving black-eyed stare.

'Oh, no! Not at all! Well, please excuse us. We have to get to the ladies' room; need to just...clean up and stuff.'

'Of course,' said the man. 'Hey, my wife Velma can escort you, make sure you're OK,' he added.

'Oh yes,' said the candyfloss woman – Rorie spotted a fleeting glance between her and her husband, and a tight little nod. 'You come right along with me, dears,' said Velma, beaming. 'I'll see you're all right.'

No, no! thought Rorie. 'Oh, that's OK,' she said

hastily. 'We'll be fine, thank you.'

'Oh, but I *insist*,' said Velma, putting her arm around Rorie. 'Come along!'

Glancing back, Rorie caught sight of the man pulling out his Shel.

Chapter 21
Theme Park

'So where you from?' asked Velma, as they passed along the boat.

'Oh, just down the coast a little way,' said Rorie, giving Elsie a surreptitious little nudge.

Then Velma said something that sounded like 'Deecey?', so Rorie just answered, 'Yes.'

'So where are your grandparents?'

'Um, at home,' said Rorie. *Grandparents?* she thought. Why not *parents?* She was dreading more questions, but at that moment they were approaching the ladies' room, and she was drowned out by the voices of a group of ten very high-spirited elderly women in matching outfits, also in need of the toilet.

'...Them pills make me go *all the time*,' said one.

'At least *you* can hold it in. *I* nearly wet meself when that boat blew up!' said another.

'Oh, don't make me laugh, I'll pee my pants!' chuckled another.

Velma grimaced and hung back, letting the women in first. Then she and the girls followed. There were three cubicles, and while these were occupied the other women formed an unwieldy mass by the sinks, chatting and laughing. It was very cramped and crowded, and there was much shuffling about as they took turns to use the toilets.

Perfect! thought Rorie, taking advantage of the situation and concealing herself behind the women. Velma, she noticed, stayed close to the door, no doubt keeping guard. Thus hidden, Rorie quickly removed the Nikki Deeds trainers, and slipped into her own shoes. Then she pulled out Aunt Irmine's jacket, put it on and hung her head low while she awaited the transformation. She glanced at Elsie's wig sitting there in the backpack. *No, don't risk it*, she thought. A wonky wig would be a dead giveaway, and she wouldn't have the chance to help Elsie put it on.

She nudged Elsie into the space under the counter unit which housed the sinks; Elsie obligingly crawled under. Not an ideal hiding place, thought Rorie, but it would have to do.

The women were now belting out a song in unison,

something about a wedding night. *No!* thought Rorie, smirking to herself. *Could one of them really be getting married?* Whatever – she was delighted they were being so rowdy.

After a few moments, she snuck a look at herself in the mirror. Yes! She was now magnificently dowdy and adult-looking. More like thirty-five than Aunt Irmine's forty-nine, but completely unrecognisable as the pretty young blonde Velma was keeping an eye out for. The backpack was the sort that could be converted into a handbag – Rorie adjusted the straps accordingly. Good. Now there was nothing to give her away.

But there was still Elsie. Rorie edged closer to Velma, who now looked decidedly aggravated, craning her neck as she tried to see past the other women. Rorie-as-Aunt-Irmine made eye contact with her. 'You looking for someone?' she asked in her newly coarse-toned voice.

'Oh, it's my granddaughter,' lied Velma. 'She's tiny, about so high,' she added, indicating with her hand. 'She was supposed to stay with her big sister, but she seems to have gone off, and may have come in here...'

'Oh, a little girl just went into the end cubicle,' said Rorie, reaching for the door handle. 'With another girl.' She leant closer conspiratorially, and jerked her head at the other women. 'Tut-tut! Noisy bunch, aren't they?'

'I'll say!' agreed Velma. 'Thank you.' As she pushed her way over to the end cubicle, Rorie leant down slightly, clicked her fingers and beckoned to Elsie, who crawled over; together, they slipped out of the door.

'OK,' said Rorie under her breath as she quick-marched Elsie away. 'We need to keep you hidden as much as possible, until we get off this boat. Now, your name is Annabel, and I'm Celia, your mum. Think you can remember that?'

'Can't I be—'

'Shh! You're *Annabel*. If we can find you a disguise, then so much the better. OK, I think this is probably just a pleasure boat, in which case there won't be ID checks when we come off...here's hoping.'

Rorie was right. Very soon after, the boat came into dock, and sure enough the crowds just spilled off. However, everyone had to filter through a narrow gap, which was attended by several uniformed officials who were scrutinising the passengers – accompanied by Velma and the silver-haired man. The officials stopped a tall blonde girl, but Velma and her husband shook their heads, and the girl was waved on.

Rorie felt as if her pounding heart would burst

through her chest as she and Elsie passed them – even though she knew she looked completely different, and that Elsie looked pretty different too, having changed into Rorie's shirt and put on an abandoned baseball cap they'd found.

But it was over in an instant – as they went by, Velma was looking at someone else, and her husband with the penetrating stare gazed right through Rorie and Elsie.

They were in.

'All right, no jumping for joy and singing about New York, OK?' warned Rorie, as they emerged onto the street.

'Oh-*kay*,' sighed Elsie heavily.

The girls had never been to New York before, but it was just as Rorie imagined it to be – if not now, then certainly some time ago, in its heyday. Skyscrapers loomed on both sides of the streets, which had steam belching out of manholes and were full of yellow cabs. In fact, Rorie noticed that these seemed to be virtually the only vehicles on the road, aside from the occasional bus and, for some reason, open horse-drawn carriage.

The smell of sizzling onions wafted over from

a nearby hot-dog stand. 'I'm starving,' said Elsie.

Rorie couldn't decide whether she was hungry or not; she was still a jumble of nerves. But she was certainly very *empty*... She reached into the bag and found her purse, then paused. 'Um, I wonder if they take euros here.'

''Course they don't!' said Elsie. 'You need dollars! Look, there's a money-changing machine over there.'

'R-i-ight.' *Well, at least this might provide some sort of clue as to where we are*, thought Rorie. She inserted a twenty-euro note, and a pile of coins came out of the bottom.

'*Silver* dollars!' squealed Elsie, delighted.

Rorie inspected the coins. They did, indeed, each say 'One Silver Dollar'. *No!* Now this was getting silly.

'Hot *dog*, hot *dog*,' chanted Elsie.

Rorie wrinkled her ugly Aunt Irmine nose. 'Ugh, no...look, there's a coffee shop. Let's get some pancakes with blueberries and maple syrup. I've always wanted to try that.'

'Yeah! An' a big tall shake!' said Elsie, measuring with her hands.

The coffee shop had red leatherette banquettes, chrome stools and squeezy bottles of ketchup and mustard on the Formica tables. It was perfect. The lady who served them wore a starched white pinny and thick make-up and sounded bored. 'Enjoy!' she commanded brusquely as she plonked steaming platefuls of fat, fluffy pancakes in front of them. She, too, was perfect, right down to the way she perched the pen behind her ear. Rorie felt as if she'd stepped back in time a hundred years. As soon as the food arrived, she realised she was famished; she and Elsie uttered not a single word to each other as they ate.

'Aah! That was the best meal I've *ever* had!' sighed Elsie, grinning blissfully.

Rorie had to admit that she too felt strangely uplifted, in spite of the terrifying experience they had just been through. Perhaps that was *why* she felt so good: they were, for now, no longer in peril. And now that her belly was filled, she could think.

'Let's just wander around for a bit,' she suggested. *That way we might be able to figure out where on earth we are*, she thought – though she didn't say that to Elsie.

Finding themselves on Broadway, they decided to follow the sign that pointed towards Times Square. But there were so many distractions. A woman in big sunglasses was practically mobbed as she tried to get from a building entrance into a waiting limousine.

Elsie nudged Rorie. 'Is she famous?'

'I *guess*...'

'Then why's she so ordinary?'

It was true – the woman was not particularly young or glamorous. Rorie shrugged. 'I've no idea.'

Elsie instantly lost interest. 'Oh, there's that pointy one!' she gasped, and Rorie turned to see the glinting stainless-steel glory of the Chrysler Building piercing the sky. They simply had to go and take a look at that. But, as with the Statue of Liberty, it seemed rather small. And the people were all wrong – still mostly elderly, and far too relaxed for the famous city that never sleeps, the Big Apple.

Because we're not *in the Big Apple*, said the words in Rorie's head. And she was more than ever convinced of this. The question was, where *were* they?

'Ooh, skating! I wanna go ice skating!' cried Elsie, as she dashed over to a nearby square, Rockefeller Plaza.

'In *June*?' But sure enough, there was a sunken rink in front of yet another tall, narrow building, full of skaters gliding around to jolly music. 'Elsie, that's all very nice, but aren't you forgetting something? We've got detective work to do.'

Elsie frowned. 'You're right.' She glanced back at the rink. 'Maybe later...'

'Yes, maybe later.'

'So what we gonna do?'

In spite of her elation, Rorie was beginning to feel weary; her aged Aunt Irmine bones were giving her trouble. 'Oh, look. Central Park's just up there,' she remarked. 'Let's go and sit on a bench and decide.'

'OK.'

They strolled up to Central Park. Rorie spotted the giant toy store, FAO Schwarz, just in time to distract Elsie and lead her a different way so she wouldn't see it. Dodging their way past scores of highly skilled rollerbladers, several street entertainers and yet more horse-drawn carriages, they found a bench beside a boating lake and sat down.

'So. What we gonna do?' asked Elsie, when she had finally finished gawping at the rollerbladers and a rather fascinating magician.

Rorie yawned. Her back was killing her. *No wonder Aunt Irmine's so miserable*, she thought. 'Oh...we'll think of something. Let's just...hang for a bit.' The warm sun filtered through the trees; it felt so wonderful to sit there, on dry land, that for now all she wanted to do was bask. She was soon fast asleep.

Elsie watched the passers-by some more, but soon grew bored. And the words *'We've got detective work to do'* were spinning around in her head. *Well, here we are in New York*, she thought. *And somewhere in this city are Mum and Dad.*

A policeman was strolling up and down the gravel path nearby. His uniform looked rather old-fashioned, she thought, like in old movies. Peaked cap, smart jacket with epaulettes, big shiny leather shoes. In fact, everything about him was shiny and old-fashioned, almost like a toytown policeman. Every now and then he doffed his hat to a passer-by, saying, 'Top o' the mornin' to ye,' in a broad Irish accent. He did seem very friendly, thought Elsie – not a bit like those scary officials at the docks. She couldn't imagine this nice man being scary at all. And he must know this place really well...

''Scuse me,' she said.

'Well, helloo there! Now ain't you a little sweetie?' said the cop, hitching up his trousers to bend down to her. 'What can I do for you, little lady?'

'Well, I was just wondering, have you seen my mum'n'dad?'

The cop glanced over at the sleeping Rorie on the bench. 'Ain't that your mammy over there?'

'Oh, no. She's my...*aunt*. My mum, right, she's got brown hair, sort of wavy, down to here – and she's ever so pretty. An' my dad—'

'Well now, I sees a lot of people every day, so I do,' interrupted the cop with a benevolent smile. 'But I'm sure your aunt must know—'

'Oh no, she doesn't!' said Elsie, shaking her head vehemently.

The sharpness of her tone woke Rorie from her sleep. As soon as she saw Elsie talking to the cop, she stood bolt upright and grabbed her by the hand.

'Oh! I, uh, didn't mean to zonk out like that...come along, *Annabel*, we've got to go. G'bye,' she said, nodding to the policeman as she began to retreat. *G'bye?* she thought, cringing as soon as she'd said it; she was sure a *real* grown-up would have said 'Good day, officer,' or something.

'Good day to you, missus,' said the cop, doffing his hat. 'But if you be looking for your sister, you know where the Big Apple meeting point is?'

'My...sister?' said Rorie, glancing uncertainly at Elsie.

'*My mum*, Aunty,' prompted Elsie, wide-eyed. 'And Dad. Remember? We lost them back there?'

'Oh! Right. Back...over there.'

'You'd best be going to the meeting point then, missus,' said the cop. He pulled out a colourful map and pointed to the spot. 'Just go down Madison till you get to the Empire State Building. It's right there, you can't miss it.'

'Well, thank you kindly, officer,' said Rorie, rather overdoing the grown-up speak now. She took the map and led Elsie away.

'Why are you talking like that?' asked Elsie, too loudly.

'Like what?'

'"Well, thank you kindly, officer,"' imitated Elsie, teasingly. 'Why you pretending you're in an ancient movie?'

'I'm not pretending anything!' said Rorie indignantly. 'But since you mention it, I *feel* as if we've stepped into an old movie, if you must know. This place – it's so phoney! You know what it reminds me of? Fashionworld...' She paused as she looked at the map. 'Oh boy. Well, that would explain it. Elsie, we're in some sort of theme park!'

Chapter 22
Barn Dance

'But this is *New York*!' insisted Elsie, now on the brink of tears.

'Elsie, look what it says on here,' said Rorie, showing her the map. Above the words 'The Big Apple' was the title 'Minimerica'.

'As in "Mini-America". Get it? It's fake!'

'Oooh!' wailed Elsie. 'How we ever gonna find Mum'n'Dad now?'

'Ssh!' said Rorie, putting an arm around her. 'Else, *please*, we really mustn't draw attention to ourselves – not after what happened on *the boat*.' She whispered these last two words, as they began to walk down 'Madison' towards the 'Empire State Building'. 'Besides, how many times do I have to tell you that we don't *know* Mum and Dad are in New York?'

Elsie said nothing. Upset though she was, she

seemed to recover remarkably quickly. By the time they reached the 'Empire State Building', she seemed almost to have forgotten she was ever upset.

Rorie, too, felt strangely calm and easily distracted. Staying focused took considerable effort. 'We're lucky that that "cop" you spoke to was really just some sort of guide, or heaven knows what might have happened to us,' she warned. 'You mustn't do that again, Elsie.'

'But he seemed so *nice...*'

'Yes, well, now you know why. What I want to know is, what kind of theme park protects itself from unauthorised visitors by trying to *kill* them? *That's* what we have to find out, Else.'

'How do we do that?'

'Well, it would help if we knew what country we were in. The currency's no help – those "silver dollars" are obviously just some kind of tokens.' Rorie studied the map again. 'All right, we know this eastern part is coastland, so if we head to the northern, western or southern edges of the park, we should be able to find out... Elsie? What is it...oh!'

Rorie followed Elsie's sightline to a large rolling-news billboard. On it was a digitally enhanced image of the two of them as they had appeared on the boat. Below it said:

204

TPs on the loose: call 0800 MINIMERICA if you see them!

'Well, at least they won't recognise *you*,' said Elsie.

'Yeah, well, I'm changing all the same. I can't stand this Aunt Irmine guise any longer; my bones ache. As for you, we'd better get you back in that wig.'

They went into a clothing store. In the changing room, Rorie removed the Aunt Irmine jacket and put on Moll's necklace. She figured she had better still have some sort of disguise, and this one was the least objectionable of them all – Moll was her own age, and she'd liked her very much. While she waited to transform, she put Elsie's second-hand baseball cap back in the backpack and fitted her with the wig. 'Now, no scratching, OK?' she warned. On the way out, a shorter, skinnier and darker Rorie spotted some free maps and took one.

'Look, this one shows the whole of Minimerica,' she said in her new, slightly husky, Moll-like voice. 'There's only like, twenty or so cities in the whole place. Seems we're near the "Brooklyn Bridge" – that'll take us straight into Washington DC, which must be where that Velma woman thought we were staying. Let's head down that way.'

As they walked through Washington DC and out the other side, Rorie had a disturbing sensation, like the opposite of waking from a bad-dream. It was like waking *into* a bad dream. And yet, as they strolled through beautiful West Virginia Park, with its deer roaming the hills, the bad-dream sensation began to fade and she felt an increasing, inexplicable sense of wellbeing.

By the time they emerged in Nashville, she found she felt almost as good as she had in the New York coffee shop. A band was playing. Lively country music filled the air and the street was teeming with dancers, young and old, expert and amateur. Everyone wore check shirts, neckerchiefs and cowboy hats; some of the women wore old-fashioned, full-skirted dresses. The oldest people sat around the edges, stamping their feet and clapping their hands for all they were worth.

Rorie and Elsie stopped to watch, and before long they too were tapping their feet – it was virtually impossible not to. The fiddler jumped down from the stage and began weaving his way among the revellers. His playing was mesmerising, fast and furious like steel wheels spinning on a railway track, and the crowd whooped and cheered.

'I'm firsty,' announced Elsie, after they'd been watching for a while.

'Oh, you should try the lemonade stand,' suggested a boy about Rorie's age nearby. 'I'm thirsty too. Here, I'll take you.' He led the way.

'Thanks,' said Rorie, following. Noticing Elsie fidgeting with her wig, she whispered, 'Stop scratching!'

'But it's *hot*!' Elsie whispered back crossly.

'You been here long?' asked the boy, glancing over his shoulder.

Rorie looked up with a broad grin. 'Not long, no.'

'I've been all over,' boasted the boy. 'We did Hollywood this morning, it was brilliant!'

Rorie spotted the chance to ask some questions. 'And you're staying with...?'

'My gran. She's in Florida at the moment. But she's done Colorado, Vegas...even Alaska! It's great there, 'cause they've got that fake snow that doesn't need cold weather. There's bears and moose – it's great!' He nodded towards Elsie, who was scratching like crazy. 'She got nits?'

'Oh yeah, *nits*!' Rorie smiled, rolling her eyes as she moved in front of Elsie and slapped her hand.

'Ow!'

'SO!' said Rorie loudly, in an attempt to cover Elsie's voice. 'Where do you live normally?' she asked, as they joined the queue at the lemonade stand.

'Milton Keynes.'

'Oh, in England.'

'Yeah.'

That wasn't much help. They had crossed water, that much Rorie knew. So surely they must be in a different country? Though she was sure they hadn't gone even as far as Wales or Ireland. It was all very confusing. 'Not from...anywhere near here then,' she fished.

'Ha ha!' laughed the boy. 'I think that's a little way off yet!'

'Right!' laughed Rorie, though she didn't understand the joke.

'What she's trying to say,' said Elsie, stepping forward, 'is where will we be when we get to the other side?'

'The other side of what?'

'Of Minimerica.'

'Well, you'll be in the water, of course!' said the boy.

'No, the *other* side,' pressed Elsie. 'The one that's not water.'

'Wow, you ain't been here long, have you?' laughed the boy.

Rorie began to feel uncomfortable. She laughed along nervously, as best she could. 'So, what? It's an island?'

The boy fell silent, and stared at her. Several other people nearby also fell silent and looked at them. Rorie could have sworn the music turned discordant.

'You're not serious?' said the boy, now deadly serious as he stepped closer and narrowed his eyes. 'You mean you really don't know?'

All of the joy and laughter in Rorie's belly was now curdling like sour milk, and she felt her cheeks burn. For a moment she was dumbfounded. 'Only joking!' she said at last, forcing a grin. 'I was just playing a game with...my cousin here. She's never been before, so I was saying there was a Mini South America and ha! She believed me!' Rorie stepped backwards, stumbling slightly. 'Oh, is that the time? We've got to get back to Granny, Annabel, she'll be wondering where we are!'

Then, trying not to hurry so much as to be obviously running off, Rorie took Elsie's hand and led her away.

Chapter 22
TP Alert

'Just keep going, and don't look back,' Rorie ordered under her breath, as they walked away from the street party. 'But no running...and no more scratching! I don't care how uncomfortable it is. Just wait till we get to a loo or something, and you can take the wig off. We *both* need to change.'

They kept going. The country music gradually faded. The girls made their way past the shoppers, the people sitting at pavement cafés. They quickened their pace.

At the edge of Nashville they came to 'Cherokee Park', where there were totem poles and wooden long houses. Still Rorie didn't look back. She was grateful for every moment that went by without a hand on her shoulder.

'I fink we're OK,' whispered Elsie eventually.

'I'm not counting on anything,' said Rorie. 'I wouldn't be surprised if that boy reported us.'

A rhythmic drumbeat pounded loudly as they drew near to the focal attraction of the park, a traditional Native American tribal dance. Elsie made a beeline for a Cherokee costume stall. 'Hey, how 'bout we get one of these?'

Rorie blanched at the price. 'They're forty dollars!'

Elsie pulled Rorie aside. 'It'd be a *perfect* disguise!' she whispered urgently.

'It also costs *money*,' Rorie replied. 'I've only got thirty dollars. I can't use the paydisc, it's too risky in this place – besides, Nolita will have cancelled it by now. Plus we have to eat, maybe find somewhere to stay...'

Elsie cast her eye around. 'Over there, then!' she said, pointing to a make-it-yourself costume stall. 'Look, those ones only cost twenty-five.'

Rorie hesitated; she would have just five dollars left over. But what could be more important than a disguise? The only alternative was shoplifting, and that *really* wasn't a good idea...

'OK,' she said at last. She would figure out later what to do about food and lodging.

The girls sat down and began to make their outfits.

While they worked, they half watched the dancing. A middle-aged white woman got up and joined in with the Native Americans, and the audience cheered. She flailed around clumsily, completely out of synch with the other dancers, but no one seemed to notice, least of all the woman herself; encouraged by the audience, she just showed off even more.

Rorie was finishing her outfit, and wondering why no one else found the spectacle as embarrassing as she did, when her heart did a flip. A boy had just sailed by and put a flyer on the table, and on it were two pictures: the original one of herself-as-Nikki-Deeds and Elsie on the boat, and another one with her in her current, Moll-like guise, apparently taken at the 'Nashville' lemonade stand. Underneath it said:

TP ALERT:
Two young females.
Last seen in Nashville.
N.B. May be in disguise!
Call 0800 MINIMERICA

Rorie turned to stone, sweating ice as she snuck a look at the stallholder. Thankfully, he hadn't seen – he was too engrossed in watching the silly woman dance.

Rorie slipped the notice into her bag.

'Look, I don't want to freak you out, but they're closing in on us,' muttered Rorie under her breath, as they walked away.

'They are?'

'Uh-huh.'

Elsie gasped at the sight of the flyer, which Rorie quickly flashed at her.

'In here,' said Rorie, pulling Elsie into the nearest restrooms. They dived into neighbouring cubicles. Rorie took off Moll's necklace, then opened up the backpack. How fast she was ploughing through her disguises! Already on number four in as many hours. But number four was Leesa Simms's cravat, and there was a major problem with that: Leesa's poor eyesight...

Suddenly, a small black furry animal darted under the partition. 'Aargh!' cried Rorie...then she saw that it was no animal, but Elsie's wig, held by Elsie's hand. 'Gimme the baseball hat!' said Elsie.

Rorie took the wig, stuffed it in the backpack and took out the baseball cap. 'No. *I'm* going to wear it. You'll just have to go as you are. At least you have a change of...ssh!' she hissed, hearing someone enter the restrooms.

Bracing herself for the plunge into the unknown, she put on the cap and a different top. Then she felt panic-stricken, as she realised there was no mirror in the cubicle. What if the cap belonged to a man? Even if it didn't, there was something very disconcerting about the prospect of emerging with no idea what she looked like... *Please let it be a girl or a woman!* she prayed, her eyes scrunched shut as she waited for the transformation. Already she was experiencing that strange, waking-into-a-bad-dream sensation, and now there was also the change. Her hands became fatter and shorter; her slants became longer on her. She felt her face. It was still mercifully soft and young, but rounder, with not much chin in evidence.

'There's no one here now,' called Elsie eventually. 'Are you ready?'

Rorie sighed. 'Yes.'

'Hey!' said Elsie, as Rorie emerged. 'You look about nine years old! Are you a boy or a girl?'

'I don't know.' Rorie glanced at herself in the mirror. *Could be worse*, she decided, with some relief.

'Where we going next, then?' asked Elsie, sounding just like any typical child in an amusement park. 'I kind of like this place! I've never heard of it, have you?'

'No, of course not.'

'I don't know why they don't advertise it. I'm sure *loads* of people would want to come!'

'Elsie, are you out of your mind? Look, I've been thinking about this a lot. That fog? It probably *surrounds* this place! They must have some kind of machines which make it. Then there's the way they jam the global positioning, all that "turn back now" business...the killer Statue of Liberty...this place is top secret, Else! Do you realise, we're probably the first "TPs" to make it on here alive? It's only because I was able to...*change*...that we're still here! Anyone else would probably be dead by now. And we're running out of time fast. But we have to find out *why* it's so secret, Else. And once we've done that...well, we have to escape. Trouble is, if Minimerica is an island, and we now have no boat...how the heck will we do that?'

Chapter 24
The Land of Elvises

They followed the sign to 'Memphis' which, judging from the crowds, was a popular destination. 'The more crowded, the better,' Rorie had decided. She was relieved to find that the bad-dream feeling was receding again.

Another news billboard glared down at them: **TP ALERT!** It was the same as the flyer – same two pictures, only a hundred times the size. Rorie's heart skipped a beat. *But you don't look like that any more!* she reminded herself. She was smaller now, and boyish-looking – though she was still unsure whether she was *meant* to be a boy or not. But she was certainly nothing like the girl – or rather *girls* – in the picture. No one would recognise her now – or Elsie, with her mousy hair and her Native American outfit.

Now Memphis loomed in front of them: big, brash, loud...and Elvissy.

'Wow, what a lot of Elvises,' remarked Elsie.

There were, indeed, many Elvises in Memphis. Everywhere they looked, there were posters of Elvis, billboards of Elvis movies, Elvis shop-signs...and Elvis music wafted on the summer breeze. As the twentieth century receded further and further into history, Elvis Presley had passed from pop icon to legend to demigod, and 'Memphis' was a massive shrine to him. Elsie's eye was drawn to a poster with a fully animated dancing Elvis on it, advertising an Elvis-a-like competition. She tried to copy the tiny Elvis moves.

Nearby was a life-size golden statue of Elvis. 'Elvis Aaron Presley,' read Rorie. 'Born 1935, Tupelo, Mississippi. Died 1977, Memphis, Tennessee, aged 42.' She gazed wistfully up at the statue's face. 'That's the same age as Dad. Else?'

Elsie was still busy with her dance moves. 'Uh-huh,' she said, not looking round.

'I said that's the same age as—'

At that moment the 'statue' turned to look at her. 'Aaargh!' she cried, and she and Elsie both ran away, screaming. But after a moment, Rorie sensed that they were not being pursued after all. She slowed her pace. 'Ah, it's all right, it's *all right*,' she reassured Elsie, clamping a hand over her mouth. 'It's only one of those painted people, like you see in London sometimes. Street entertainers. See?'

Elsie looked. Sure enough, the golden man was still on his plinth. He winked. Elsie quietened down. 'Ooh...what *is* it with this place and statues?'

'Wow, what a great start,' said Rorie. 'Let's *really* try not to draw attention to ourselves now, OK?'

'OK.'

They wandered on, admiring the broad, open-topped Cadillacs in milkshake pink and peppermint green that cruised by, chrome glinting in the sunlight.

Elsie stared. 'People really used to drive around in things like that?'

'Yeah – you've seen them in movies, Else.'

'Wow. This place is like Fashionworld – only with old people,' remarked Elsie, as they passed yet another elderly man with slicked-back silver hair and blue suede shoes.

'Mmm...hey, there's a gift shop,' said Rorie. 'Let's take a look. Maybe there'll be some...guides to Minimerica, or something. Might give us some clues.'

But the shop only had Elvis gifts. Rorie searched for something useful, but found nothing. She was about to leave, when she heard a man call, 'Hey, Victor!' A heavy-set man with a silver quiff had apparently just spotted an old acquaintance.

'Ed? Hey, good to see you!' said the other shorter, bald-headed man. 'I was wondering when I'd bump into you. Max told me you'd retired. How long you been here?'

'Oh, only about a week,' said Ed. 'Man, it feels good to be back! I couldn't wait, I tell you.'

'Does that to you, doesn't it?'

'Aah, it's been too long,' said Victor, a blissful look on his face. 'Soon as I got here, it was like happiness running through my veins – it's the only way I can describe it.'

'Oh yeah, I know *exactly* what you mean,' said Ed, nodding. Rorie snuck a glance at him while pretending to study a book on Elvis sightings. His smile was so blissful, it was almost spooky. He let out a sigh of satisfaction. 'Best bosses in the world, without a doubt.'

'Yeah, who else gives you all this?' agreed Victor.

'Well, we wouldn't actually know if anyone did really, would we?' said Ed, with a wink.

'Oh, I think Rexco would!'

Rorie nearly dropped the book. *Rexco!* She fumblingly replaced it on the shelf and looked around for Elsie.

Elsie seemed oblivious, apparently too busy browsing on the display of 'Elvis talismans'. 'Look, Rorie,' she said, pointing to a necklace. 'It's made with real Elvis hair!'

'Wow,' said Rorie, not really hearing. She gave Elsie a discreet nudge, then hushed her and strained to hear more of the conversation. The men had apparently moved on to discussing their families.

'...Our Nina, she's been with the firm a year now,' Victor was saying.

'Oh, so she's about due for her first holiday here, then?'

'Any day now, actually, looking forward to seeing her. To be honest with you, it won't be before time. She's been a bit difficult of late, asking awkward questions, that sort of thing. Got doubts about her job.'

'Ah, don't worry,' said Ed. 'Coming here will change all that.'

'Yeah, that's what I hear...'

After that, the two men fell to discussing meeting

up for dinner with their wives. Rorie decided to move on.

'Excuse me,' said the lady behind the counter, just as Rorie was leaving. Rorie felt a jolt of anxiety, before the woman added sternly, 'Would you put that back, please?' and Rorie realised she was still clutching a pendant with a tuft of the 'Real Elvis Hair' attached to it.

'Oh, pardon me, ma'am,' said Rorie, replacing the necklace on its stand. Then she froze. Her voice was deeper! And American! And 'ma'am'? She'd never used the term 'ma'am' in her entire life! In fact, if it weren't too preposterous, she could swear she had sounded like...no! Surely not.

Rorie put her head down and, taking Elsie by the hand, swiftly exited the shop. 'Elsie,' she hissed under her breath, as they moved hurriedly on. 'Do I look different to you?'

'Well, 'course you do, with that hat.'

'No, I mean different from that...you know what I mean!'

Elsie peered at her. 'Oh, hang on, yeah. Weren't your eyes a bit squinty before? And I fink your nose...'

'Oh boy, you realise what just happened?' said Rorie, her voice beginning to revert to how it was before. 'I was starting to change back there, from holding onto that stupid Elvis-hair thing!'

'Hey! You mean *hair* works the same as cloves?'

'Well...' Rorie thought; she remembered how she had instinctively used the hair from Nolita's hairbrush when she'd been trying to access her computer files. And it had worked. 'Yes, now you mention it, seems it does...what?'

Elsie had come to a halt, and was gaping at Rorie like a goldfish.

'What? What's happening now?' Rorie felt her face.

'Oh, Rorie!' was all Elsie could manage, her voice full of awe and wonder.

'Elsie, what is it?'

'You can be the *real Elvis*.'

'What? You believe that nonsense? Oh, Else, don't be daft. It's just some cheap gimmick!'

'No, it's not, it's real!'

'Oh sure, and this is really America,' said Rorie sarcastically, marching ahead.

'It is!' insisted Elsie. 'I mean, no, I know this isn't America, but the *hair's* real. It said so.'

'Else, it's just any old person's hair. Elvis is long gone! Besides, how much hair do you think one person can have? There were stacks of those things!'

'It's *real*, I tell you – they used his actual Dina.'

'Dina? Oh, you mean DNA.'

'Yeah, that's it. It said on the display thingy, they growed it in a lab-or-a-to-rory.'

'They –' Rorie paused, as she grasped exactly what this meant. DNA implants…grown in a laboratory…it *was* possible! 'Oh my God!' She grabbed hold of Elsie's arm. 'Then it's real!'

'Du-uh!' Elsie practically yelled. 'That's what I've been *saying*. Yes, it's real.'

Chapter 25
Good Luck Charm

On an open-air stage nearby, a very short man in a white jumpsuit was murdering a perfectly good Elvis song, 'Stuck on You', – or rather, 'Stugg-own-yew'.

'That's the competition!' exclaimed Elsie. 'The one I saw the poster for, with the dancing Elvis...you could win! Oh, Rorie, you should go and buy one of those Elvis-hair thingies. They only cost forty-two dollars, go on!'

'Are you crazy? I'm not doing that! Besides, we can't afford it.'

'But—'

'Now listen, did you get what those guys were saying back there?'

'Yeah...I mean no, not really. Oh, Rorie, come on! You—'

'No!' snapped Rorie. 'Look, have you completely

forgotten what we're trying to do here?'

'No, but if—'

'*Detective work*, Elsie. And what do you think those men were talking about? *Rexco.* I think this place is just one giant playground for Rexco workers. And we need to find out exactly why it's such a big secret.'

'Then use it as a disguise,' suggested Elsie.

Rorie groaned. 'You're not listening!'

'Well, you're running out of disguises. Plus it's *worth* it,' argued Elsie. 'You'd win a lot of prize money!'

'I don't care, I... Really?'

'That's what I've been *trying* to tell you. I saw it on the poster!'

The tiny Elvis had left the stage, and now a big, bearded guy, also in a white jumpsuit, was warbling, '*It's now or never...*' He was terrible. This, it seemed, was the very same Elvis-a-like competition that the poster had been advertising. With big prize money. Elsie did seem to have a point...but no, it really wouldn't do; they *had* to stay undercover.

'*It's now or never*,' sang the bearded Elvis again, seemingly joining forces with Elsie in urging Rorie to act. She was reminded of something she'd once heard, about a woman who claimed the spirit of Elvis appeared to her the night before her wedding, singing 'Devil in Disguise' and 'Heartbreak Hotel'. This so convinced the woman that the marriage was doomed that she decided not to go through with it. It now occurred to Rorie that such a disguise could be really powerful...

'All right,' she said at last. 'I'll get it...*if* we have enough money.'

'Yay!' cried Elsie.

'Shh!' They sat down, and Rorie counted out her silver dollars and euros. 'Right, for twenty euros I got thirty "dollars". I only have six dollars left, but I have...thirty more euros.'

'Well, that'll be loads, won't it?' asked Elsie.

Rorie sighed. 'Not *loads*...I really won't have much left over at all. And I don't know about you, but I'm getting hungry. But...OK, I'm going to do it. But only if you promise to keep quiet, right?'

'I promise.'

Rorie changed the money, then strode boldly into the shop and bought the necklace. 'All right,' she said, as they left for the second time. 'I'm going to try this out, but not in the ladies' room. Don't want to freak anyone out. Over there, in those bushes.'

They settled down amid a trio of rhododendron shrubs. In the distance, another lousy Elvis impersonator was singing 'Be My Little Good Luck Charm' as Rorie removed the baseball cap in preparation for her change.

'You never do combinations,' observed Elsie.

'Well, why should I?'

'I dunno. What if you put on everything at once? That hat, Nikki Deeds's shoes, Aunt Irmine's jacket, Moll's necklace, Leesa Simms's cravat and Elvis's hair?'

'I'm *not* about to find out!'

'But just imagine,' said Elsie, her voice getting louder, 'you might be like, this old lady who does amazing stunts, is a computer wizard who can break codes and sings like Elvis!'

'Elsie, shut up!'

'Sorry.'

Rorie took the Elvis necklace out of its box. It was a simple chain with a pendant in the form of a decorative clasp; hanging from that was the lock of hair, dark brown, about two centimetres long. It looked so ordinary, thought Rorie, as she brushed it over her palm like a paintbrush. Then, hands trembling, she put it on, tucking it inside her shirt so it would be next to her skin. Panic-stricken, she suddenly wondered whether she would turn into the young, good-looking Elvis, or the much less healthy forty-year-old one? *Well, you've gone and bought it now*, she told herself. *You have to give it a try.*

Rorie shut her eyes. *Here I am*, she thought, *a fugitive on a secret fog-hidden island, risking my life to find out what happened to my parents, and now I'm turning into Elvis. Or Elv-ish, at least... Could life get any weirder?*

The sensation, after a moment or two, was unmistakable – yet more powerful this time. Stuff was hard at work inside her – cells were mutating, multiplying. Blood rushed furiously through her veins, and she felt vaguely headachy and nauseous. She clutched at her belly and groaned.

'Rorie, are you all right?' asked Elsie.

'I...don't know,' said Rorie. She opened her eyes and saw the hem of her slants ride up her hairy shins, felt the pull of her T-shirt across her shoulders. But she was relieved to note that the waistband, though expanded, did not strain. Finally, the discomfort began to ease. She sighed with relief. 'How do I look?' she asked, noticing with a small thrill the rich, round darkness in her voice.

Elsie peered at her. 'Wow,' she gasped. '*Definitely*
Elvissy.'

Rorie pulled out her tiny hand-mirror, and
inspected what she could. 'Oh my God!' she gasped,
running her fingers along her lengthened jawline. She
turned sideways, admiring the simple elegance of her
profile, with its dark, perfectly drawn brows, the hint
of chubbiness in the cheeks, the Cupid's-bow lips. Her
hair was still rather longer than Elvis's own, making
her look more like a female version of Elvis than the
singer himself. Instinctively, she swept it back off her
face. She would have admired herself some more, but
suddenly a large, excitable black dog collided with her,
knocking the mirror from her hand, and began
barking at them.

'Sshhh! Nice doggy! Sshhh!' hissed Elsie, but the
dog wouldn't shut up.

Woof! Woof! Woof!

'*You ain't nothin' but a hound dog*,' came the
strangulated sound from the stage.

'Let's get outta here!' said Rorie-as-Elvis, and she
and Elsie scrambled out the other side of the bushes.

They plunged headlong into two men in official
uniform. 'Whoa there!' said one of them, looking

Rorie up and down curiously, taking in the ill-fitting clothing. 'Just conducting some routine spot checks,' he added, his ugly pizza-face red and sweaty in the sun. 'May I see your ID, please?'

Chapter 26
Gold Lamé Suit

'Well, I, uh…' Rorie-as-Elvis faltered. She studied the ground in front of her. Her mouth was dry as paper, her throat constricted.

'She…hasn't got it on her,' Elsie said. 'At the moment. Have you?'

'Uh, no,' Rorie mumbled.

'It's at home,' added Elsie, helpfully.

Speak! Rorie told herself. 'Uh-huh,' was all she could manage.

'We can go back an' get it, can't we?' suggested Elsie, nudging her. It was obvious she thought this might be a good ruse and they could just run away.

Oh yeah, as if, thought Rorie.

The officer's eyes narrowed, and his voice hardened. 'I'm afraid we can't allow that, young lady. As everyone on Minimerica knows, you gotta keep your ID on you at *all* times.'

Rorie felt the hairs bristle on the back of her neck. 'Truth of the matter is, sir,' she said at last, still startled by her own rich, baritone voice. 'I…I lost it. I'm waitin' for a replacement.'

Pizza-Face was not amused. 'Since when?'

'Since this afternoon.'

The official took out his Shel. 'What time did you report it?'

Rorie mentally kicked herself – of course he would check! The song 'Suspicious Minds' warbled away in the distance. 'Oh, it was only just a short while ago,' she replied, suppressing the Elvis accent as much as she could. 'Probably didn't go through yet.'

Pizza-Face gave her a withering look. 'It "goes through" instantaneously. Name?'

The name 'Elvis' popped into Rorie's head, but she stopped herself just in time. *Not Rorie, either*, she told herself. 'Celia,' she said at last.

The officer didn't flinch. Rorie was relieved that apparently she could still pass for a girl.

'Celia who?' he asked.

Rorie tried to think, but panic had wiped her mind blank. Could she get away with 'Silk'? No! But perhaps… 'Celia Slick,' she said. 'S–L–I–C–K.'

The man punched it in, then waited. 'Got a Darren Slick here…no Celia. You're not registered.'

'*Caught in a trap*,' went the song.

The other officer, a narrow-faced man with an unnerving squint, took out some handcuffs.

'Who's the kid?' asked Pizza-Face.

'She's my sister,' said Rorie. 'Uh, Annabel Slick.'

'She'll have to come along too.'

Rorie thought she would faint. 'Come along? Where?'

Pizza-Face pocketed his Shel. 'This is a serious matter. The superintendent will deal with you right away. You know what happens to TPs.'

Rorie saw again in her mind's eye the descending arm of the 'Statue of Liberty'… the exploding boat…

The handcuff was clamped around Rorie's wrist. A crowd of onlookers had gathered to watch, enjoying the spectacle of the caught TPs.

'No, please, you mustn't!' cried Elsie.

'Oh, but we *have* to.'

'But you don't know who she is!' Elsie yelled. 'Give her a go on the stage, she'll show you!'

Rorie wanted the ground to swallow her up. At the very least, she wanted to say, 'Hang on, we haven't tested the singing voice yet!'

233

But when Pizza-Face just said, 'Dream on,' and his accomplice fastened the handcuffs, she realised she had nothing to lose. 'Oh, please, sir,' she begged, her voice growing squeaky with anxiety. 'You can get all the reinforcements you like – I can't get away, I know that. Just let me do this one thing before I go with you.'

'Nothin' doing,' insisted Pizza-Face, and he took hold of Elsie's wrist. Elsie wriggled, squirmed and squealed, but she was helpless in his grip. More and more people had gathered to stare.

This is it, thought Rorie, as Squint-Eyes led her away under the gloating gaze of the onlookers. *We've had it.*

Still Elsie kicked and screamed for all she was worth. 'But she's Elvis!' she yelled.

'Sure she is,' said Pizza-Face. 'And I'm the Queen of Sheba!'

Rorie caught the eye of a woman in the crowd, who then turned and whispered to her neighbour. *Oh yeah*, thought Rorie, seething with resentment. *You're really enjoying this, aren't you?* But just as she thought this, Rorie realised something: she had an audience.

'*Uh-uh-huh, uh-huh, yay-yeah!*' she drawled, singing the opening bars of Elvis's 'All Shook Up'. The

234

woman did a double-take. Rorie repeated it, then curled her lip in classic Elvis-style.

'Hey! Whaddaya think you're doing?' snapped Squint-Eyes.

'She IS Elvis!' screamed Elsie.

'Hey!' called out another onlooker. 'She's good! Put her on the stage, go on!'

Squint-Eyes just yanked harder; the steel cut into Rorie's wrist. She sang on, defiant.

'Hey, what's the matter with you?' jeered another man at the officers. 'Let her do her act.'

'Yeah, *then* you can do her in,' called another one.

'She's the *real* Elvis,' Elsie kept saying, whipping the growing crowd into a lather. Soon they were all calling for Rorie to perform, and getting in the way of the officers' progress.

'All right!' yelled Pizza-Face, grinding to a halt. 'Five minutes, that's all you got.' He talked into his Shel, calling for reinforcements. 'But the second you're off that stage,' he warned, wagging a finger in Rorie's face, 'you're done for.'

The sun was low in the sky. Backstage, about thirty Elvises of all shapes and sizes milled around, all dressed in rhinestone-studded white flared jumpsuits.

Rorie paced up and down, still handcuffed to Squint-Eyes. 'Nervous, huh?' he said jeeringly. 'Jailhouse Rock' shrieked away in the background.

Rorie felt her belly rumble, and she realised she was desperate for a peanut butter and banana sandwich – nothing else would do. No sooner had she thought this than a brightly made-up young woman with bouffant hair approached, offering a tray full of peanut butter and banana sandwiches. 'Care to try one?' she simpered.

Rorie gaped at her. 'You're kiddin' me!'

'Oh no, these were Elvis's favourite; they're on the house. Give you plenty of energy!'

Elvis's favourite. *No wonder I was craving one*, thought Rorie. Normally the anxiety would have killed her appetite...and she had never had a peanut butter and banana sandwich in her life before. 'Thank you very much,' she murmured, taking two with her free hand.

'Hey, that's very good!' said the woman, laughing.

'Huh?' said Rorie, stuffing a sandwich into her mouth.

'The accent! Very good!'

Squint-Eyes peered meanly at Rorie. 'How'd you *do* that?'

Rorie shrugged. The sandwich was delicious; it comforted her somehow, and made her feel less queasy. Elsie helped herself to a handful as well.

Just then the woman spotted the handcuffs, and her manner instantly became more guarded. 'Ah, you're the late entry, aren't you?' She turned to Squint-Eyes. 'Is she allowed to change into an outfit?'

'No, ma'am, thank you,' said Rorie hastily, through a peanutty, banana-ey mouthful. Now she was maxing out the Elvis voice, and beginning to enjoy it. But a used outfit was out of the question; it could completely mess up her performance.

The woman surveyed Rorie's ill-fitting slants and shirt. 'Well, it's kind of required.'

Rorie realised her outfit did look a bit ridiculous. 'Uh, you got any new ones, not worn before? I'm sorry, ma'am, I got a bit of a thing about hygiene.'

'Well, the white jumpsuits are the most popular, but I'm sure we can find you something else.'

As the evening sun glowed on the horizon, more crowds gathered to enjoy the spectacle. Minimerica officials were all over the place like a swarm of locusts. Still guarded by the two men, but free of the handcuffs, Rorie stood in the wings, knees trembling beneath the trousers of her gold lamé suit.

'Well, now, news travels fast in Minimerica,' announced the compere. 'And I know you will have heard about the TPs who were captured a little while ago.'

The crowd cheered rapturously at the capture of the enemy.

Rorie clutched her hand. 'Oh, Else, they hate me!'

'No, they *don't*,' insisted Elsie. 'They only think they do. Don't forget who you are! Knock 'em dead.'

'Before she is hauled away for questioning,' the compere went on, 'she has asked to perform for us. So, please welcome – Celia Slick!' There were boos and jeers from the audience. Pizza-Face gave Rorie a shove in the back, and she stumbled onto the stage, blinking in the spotlights as the drums started up. Immediately, flying objects – sandwiches, fruit, drinks pouches – were pelting her from all angles. She ran off, screaming.

'OK, now ladies and gentlemen, ladies and gentlemen!' cried the compere, waving his arms about, as the backing group halted the music. The boos subsided. 'Now, now, you've heard of a condemned man's last wish,' the compere went on. 'So please grant this young lady hers. No heckling please, and no missiles. Once again – Celia Slick!' He retreated. The band started up again, and Rorie strode on, determined not to give Pizza-Face the satisfaction of shoving her this time.

And as she returned to the blaze of lights, all the anger – towards the audience, towards Rexco, towards Uncle Harris...and yes, towards Nolita – came out in full force with a great big 'YOU AIN'T NOTHIN' BUT A HOUND DOG!'

The band followed suit, and she was away. It was in her, the song, the moves, every inflection; she was *possessed*. She yelled, shrieked and growled, and shivered all over as if in a fever. Her slicked-back hair fell forward across her face. 'WELL, YOU AIN'T NEVER CAUGHT A RABBIT, YOU AIN'T NO FRIEND OF MINE!' This was the cue for the band to play the instrumental interlude. Meanwhile, Rorie knew just what moves to make. She rocked back and forth, rolled forward on tiptoes, knees bent, arms akimbo. She trembled, she struck poses; she even allowed herself a little half-smile at the audience. She was having the time of her life.

The song ended.

The audience were silent.

Rorie gazed out at them. *Well, that's that*, she

thought. *Now I am to die.*

Then, out of nowhere, there came a deafening roar. It took Rorie a moment to realise what it was: applause. Rapturous applause.

Chapter 27
Max Bix

The audience clamoured for more. The band prompted Rorie to do another number, so she launched into 'Blue Suede Shoes'. The audience went berserk.

Still the fire burnt inside Rorie, spurring her on with a passion. She glittered and glowed under the lights, suddenly the adored golden girl-boy. She felt powerful – and spitting with anger – the whole thing coming as naturally to her as if – well, as if she'd been singing it all her life. It felt as if the song had been written just for her, just for that moment. They could knock her down, step in her face...they could do anything, but they couldn't touch her 'blue suede shoes'. Maybe they weren't blue, or suede, but the meaning was the same. She had her Nikki Deeds trainers. She had the Elvis-hair necklace. No matter what happened, she still had her secret, that she was a human chameleon. Yes, she still had that...

Rorie belted out the last line, and as the guitar plucked out the final bars of the song, on came Pizza-Face and Squint-Eyes, ready to take her away.

The audience – who, as with all of Minimerica, were mostly elderly – surged creakily forward as fast as they could and, not caring about their stiff knees and dodgy backs, began clambering up onto the stage. The army of security men sprang into action, quickly forming a human barrier to control the excited pensioners.

Now the handcuffs were on again, and Rorie was being led off.

'Stop!' cried Elsie, grabbing hold of the microphone. 'Everybody, quiet! I have an announcement to make! QUI-I-I-ET!'

The audience simmered down.

'OK! Now!' Elsie took a couple of deep breaths. 'You have just seen my sister do a brilliant Elvis impersonation, right?'

Howls and whoops from the audience.

'All right, well listen: that's because—'

'Elsie...Annabel, no!' cried Rorie, lurching forward. She was instantly yanked back by Squint-Eyes.

Elsie ignored her. 'Because she *is* Elvis... reincarnated!'

Once again, the audience went wild. Rorie could swear they believed it.

'And...*and*,' Elsie called out over the clamour, '...we're orphans. It's true we're not s'posed to be here, but we ran away from the children's home 'cause we were scared for our lives! We were beaten every night – my sister 'specially, 'cause they thought she was weird... I ask you, is that any way to treat the King?'

The audience were with her a hundred per cent; they protested loudly at such treatment.

Oh wow, thought Rorie. Elsie was off again with her wild imaginings, believing her own fiction. But this time Rorie was grateful – even though she wasn't sure where all this was going.

'She might look grown-up, ladies and gentlemen, but she's just a kid! She's really only—'

'Seventeen,' interrupted Rorie. 'Nearly eighteen.' Having tried out a couple of adult guises by now, she realised that the independence she might have if people *thought* she was an adult could be valuable.

'All right, now,' said a tall, silver-haired man, striding onstage with a very distinguished-looking brunette lady at his side. The man took the microphone. 'Ladies and gentlemen,' he announced in a Texan twang. 'I think we got ourselves a winner here, don't you?'

The audience roared its approval.

The man turned to Rorie and shook hands with her vigorously. 'I'm Max Bix, I run Minimerica, and this here's my good lady wife, Lonnie. My, my! I never thought I believed in carnations before, but this is somethin' else. Somethin' else!'

'*Re*incarnation, Max,' corrected Lonnie discreetly.

Max gazed at Rorie with an expression of almost religious reverence, which made Rorie want to look just about anywhere but back at him. 'Miss, that's one fine act you got there, for sure...uncanny!' He turned once again to the audience. 'Now, everybody. Here at Minimerica we're tough on TPs, I think you appreciate that. But I don't know about you, I'm wonderin' if we don't have a special case here...'

The audience cheered loudly.

Max Bix beamed back at them, clearly enjoying the popularity of his idea. After a while, Lonnie nudged him, and his expression instantly changed to one of stern importance. 'Ahem, of course, we will need to make security checks...'

'The King lives!' cried one man, and this set off

a round of chants: 'The King lives, the King lives!'

'*As I have said*,' pronounced Max loudly, 'I'm prepared to make this a special case...' The audience calmed down a little. '...On the condition that this young, uh, *lady*, is contracted to remain here in Maximerica – I mean, *Minimerica* – and perform regularly for the good people of our nation – uh, *leisure island*.'

Once again, there was rapturous applause.

'Anybody here *object* to my plan?' asked Max.

The audience fell silent. Squint-Eyes stepped forward. 'Mr Bix, sir, you can't break the rules for someone just 'cause they think they're Elvis. It's not fair!' The audience began to boo him.

'Well, I, uh, think that when you're in charge, you can make the rules up as you go along,' said Max. 'That's why I took this job, anyhow,' he added with a smirk.

Sensing unease among the audience at this remark, Lonnie grabbed the microphone. 'What my husband means is that the buck stops with him.'

'Yes, and make no mistake,' added Max, taking the mike back, 'I think very carefully about my decisions, always got the very best interests of Max – er, *Mini*merica at heart. Right, Celia, you and your sister are coming with me. G'bye, everybody!' He waved, and gestured for Squint-Eyes to unshackle Rorie.

As the crowd cheered, Rorie was so mixed up inside, she didn't know whether to be glad or not. No matter how much she had enjoyed performing, the thought of being trapped on Minimerica, and having to repeat it over and over again, was like a nightmare. And the verging-on-religious devotion she seemed to have inspired made her feel positively queasy. But she decided to worry about that later; for now, she and Elsie appeared to be safe.

'Lonnie bakes the best chicken pot pie, don't you, hon?' said Max, as Lonnie brought the pie to the dinner table.

'I sure do!' agreed Lonnie, beaming proudly.

The house – which, as it turned out, was the mini White House, back in 'Washington DC' – was all done out in pastel colours and furniture so highly polished that Rorie could see her face – or rather *Elvis's* face – in it. Max and Lonnie's three children, Bonnie, Benjy and Bud, sat like little angels at the table, hair smooth as silk.

'You know somethin'?' said Max, delving into his pie. 'There's been reports lately of two girls gone missing in Europe-Land... What, Lonnie?'

'It's *England*, honey,' Lonnie pointed out, smiling sweetly.

'Oh, right, that little island part off the edge, uh-huh,' said Max. 'Lonnie does like to be pacific about things.'

'*Specific*, honey,' said Lonnie.

'See what I mean? Well now, anyhow, these two girls...nobody knows where they went. And now here you two are. Kinda different from those two girls, yet...kinda the same, and all. One of you, anyhow. Now, ain't that the darndest thing!'

'Oh, they drowned, that's what I heard,' mentioned Benjy, who was about ten, casually.

'Really?' gasped Rorie and Elsie in unison.

'Well, sure. There were two other girls saw it happen. Some accident with a jet ski, crashed into the rocks, *pchhoom!* Swimming with the fishies now.'

Rorie and Elsie looked at each other. *Nikki Deeds and Leesa Simms.* Lying, no doubt, to cover up for their failure to finish off their victims.

'Now, Benjy, we don't know that,' Lonnie cautioned. 'No bodies have been found. And it's not nice to enjoy others' misfortune, honey.'

'You know what the buzz is around these parts?' said Max. 'They're saying it's a miracle. That you just appeared out of the sea, like...like...'

'Like Venus, Dad,' prompted Bonnie, the eldest.

'She emerged fully formed from the sea, daughter of Neptune.'

'Thank you, Bonnie,' said Max. He shrugged. 'But of course, that's impossible! Am I right, Celia?'

Rorie thought she saw a flicker of something in his eyes, as if he genuinely wasn't sure. 'Well, I—'

'I told you, we ran away from the children's home,' Elsie cut in. 'We just got in a rowing boat and we wanted to go to…Ireland, but we ended up here an' the boat got 'sploded.'

Max waved it away. 'Well, well, all in good time. We can discuss more tomorrow. One thing I do know is I never saw anything like that performance of yours tonight, Celia – sent shivers down my spine. You'd be a real asset to the nation – uh, to Minimerica. I don't mind telling you, I'd like to have you stay on incertainly—'

'*Indefinitely*, honey,' said Lonnie.

'Indefinitely; that is to say, for good. What do you say, Celia? You'd be well cared for in every respect.'

Lonnie gently touched her husband's arm. 'Honey? I think maybe they need to get some sleep. They look so tired!'

'Oh. Sure,' said Max. 'Guess we can take care of business tomorrow.'

Rorie suddenly felt immensely grateful. Fatigue was settling into her bones like hardening clay. Yet one question had been raging in her head all the while, and it was only now that she felt bold enough to ask it. 'Uh, Mr Bix, sir,' she ventured in her Elvis-Tennessee drawl as she stood up to leave. 'We're on an island, right?'

'You got it,' beamed Max.

'Uh, you mind telling me which one?'

'Well, Minimerica, of course.'

Rorie rubbed her forehead. 'Well, yeah, but...OK, *before* it was Minimerica? See, I don't recall any island in the Celtic Sea...'

Max and Lonnie exchanged meaningful glances. 'How old did you say you were, Celia?' asked Max at last.

'Seventeen.'

Max gave Rorie a patronising smile that set her teeth on edge. 'Sweetheart, there's some things you don't get to learn about in high school geography lessons. Now you go on up to bed.' His eyes twinkled.

Rorie woke to find Elsie nudging her. 'Wake *up*, Rorie!'

Rorie groaned and sat up. She had taken off the

Elvis pendant – no matter how risky, there was no way she was going to spend the night as Elvis. 'Blimey, twelve o'clock!' she exclaimed, consulting her watch. She fell back on the pillow.

'Get up, I'm starving!' moaned Elsie, pulling on her arm.

'All right, all *right*! You're always starving.' Rorie yanked her arm back and flopped over. 'Just be patient, OK? That was hard work yesterday.'

'You only did two songs!'

'Elsie! It puts a lot of strain on the body, all that changing, you know. And this one was really intense for some reason. Plus I was Elvis for, what? Four hours or something. Do you have *any* idea how exhausting that is?'

'And now you gotta be him again.'

'I can't. I'm shattered. I'm not leaving this room. Go tell them I'm not to be disturbed. I can't even begin to get my head around how we're going to get out of here. But we're *going* to, somehow.'

Elsie trotted downstairs to find that Max and the kids were all out. Nobody was in the kitchen either. A gentle thrumming sound came from down the hall. Elsie followed it, and found Lonnie sitting in front of an array of computer screens.

'Hi!' Elsie said brightly.

Lonnie let out a little yelp. 'Oh, my goodness!' she gasped, spinning round in her chair. 'I didn't hear you!' She looked quite different from last night. Her soft, wavy hair was pulled tightly back off her face, and she wore glasses. The effect was very business-like. 'Well, you girls certainly were tired, weren't you!' she said, pulling off the glasses. 'Let me rustle up some breakfast for you. Where's Celia?'

'Oh, she's gonna just sleep all day,' said Elsie.

Lonnie looked concerned. 'Oh, I hope she's OK...well, why don't you take something up for her, and I'll look in on her in a while.' She shut down the computer, turned off the lights and left the room. Elsie noticed the door close with the sort of *clunk* that you only get with high-security doors, like some of the ones at Poker Bute Hall. She followed Lonnie into the kitchen. Lonnie put on her pinny and was instantly transformed into the perfect homemaker from last night. 'I was going to go to Hollywood today, and was thinking I would take you two along,' she said, fetching eggs and milk from the fridge. 'But if Celia's not up to it, I don't know—'

'Oh, she'll be OK here by herself,' said Elsie quickly. 'I'd love to come!'

Lonnie gave her a sideways look. 'Well...we can't be too careful, you know. There'll have to be security guards.'

'She won't mind,' insisted Elsie.

'OK,' said Lonnie at last. 'We'll leave after you've eaten.'

Rorie finished off the last of her French toast and gazed out of the window; there were Pizza-Face and Squint-Eyes, patrolling up and down outside. It made her feel like a prisoner – yet this didn't trouble her in the least. In fact, she could hardly believe her luck. Because there were no guards *inside* the house, and, thanks to Elsie, she now knew all about the computer room. As soon as the cleaner left – Rorie could hear her vacuuming downstairs – she would have a fantastic opportunity to snoop.

As soon as the cleaner left.

Rorie waited. The vacuuming stopped, but there were still the sounds of someone bustling about. Rorie looked at the time; it was already one o'clock. Surely she would leave soon? She wished she'd found out what time she'd be going, By three o'clock she had just begun to wonder if the cleaner wasn't actually there as an unofficial extra guard, when she heard the front door slam. She peered through the window and watched her leave. *Yes!* At last.

She took the Moll necklace, the Leesa Simms cravat and the Elvis pendant (for quick changes, if necessary), put them in her pocket and went downstairs. Near the front door were Lonnie's slippers, reassuringly old and worn. Rorie took a deep breath. She realised she had begun to dread these transformations; the last one had taken so much out of her. *Just do it*, she told herself, and made herself put them on. She sat down on the elegant blue damask settee and waited for the change.

The slippers were too big for Rorie but, with painful inevitability, her feet soon began to fill them. She was reminded of a dream she had once had, of a pair of impossibly gigantic shoes she had been expected to fill. Then she remembered with intense irritation Max's remark the night before, about how a mere schoolgirl like herself needn't worry her little head about exactly what island Minimerica was on... Perhaps now she would find out.

Her head ached, and her veins pulsated painfully. Rorie clenched her fists and scrunched up her eyes. *It's worth it, it's worth it!* she told herself. Then the pain began to ease. Finally, she inspected her Lonnie-fied appearance in the hall mirror with the usual mixture of satisfaction, awe and mild revulsion – though for once the change wasn't too dramatic; Lonnie had similarly thick, dark hair, and generous lips like Rorie. Only the maturity, the squarer jaw and closer-set eyes gave away the change. Taking Lonnie's pinny from the kitchen, Rorie found her way to the computer room. She punched out the security code which popped into her head, and opened the door.

Now for the hard part. This would be the same as Nolita's computer: a fingerprint would be required. It was for this reason that Rorie had brought the pinny – well washed and starched, it nevertheless carried the tired sheen of something routinely worn day after day over some considerable time. Having started up the computer and given the password, Rorie wrapped her right hand in the pinny, then shut her eyes and focused all her thoughts on her right thumb. As with Nolita's computer, she just had to guess the right moment to take the plunge – yet this time she felt she knew when the tingling warmth in her thumb had reached its pinnacle. As prompted by the computer, she pressed her thumb to the sensor pad.

'*Welcome, Lonnie.*'

The four screens connected to the computer filled

up with data and images. Rorie was momentarily bewildered; having all the Lonnie-ness concentrated in her right thumb meant her brain didn't connect with what she was seeing at first. But gradually it began to make sense to her, and she knew what each screen related to. One concerned general matters to do with the maintenance of Minimerica. Another was 'Staff', containing a list of vacancies and applicants for jobs on Minimerica. The other two concerned 'Visitors – Short Term', and 'Residents'.

She dived straight into the 'General' section, eager to solve the big Minimerica mystery: where *were* they? The answer, when at last she made sense of all the data relating to current coordinates, rate of acceleration, etc., was astonishing: currently in the Celtic Sea, the island was moving in a northwesterly direction. *Moving?* How was that possible? Finding a file called 'Structural Survey', she opened it up. At first the graphics were confusing – lots of cross-sections at various points, showing data relating to maintenance. But when Rorie zoomed in on the submarine levels, it all became clear: Minimerica was a man-made, floating island.

The magnitude of this discovery was such that Rorie could barely contemplate anything else for a moment. But she had to move on; she couldn't afford to squander her time. Why did people come here? Were they made to, or did they visit by choice? Why were they mostly old people? And what was it about Minimerica, anyhow, that seemed to have such a mesmerising effect on people?

Chapter 29
Military Muscle

Remembering the conversation she had overheard between the two men in the shop, Rorie decided to check in on the short-term visitors. She remembered that one of the men was called Victor – though of course she didn't know his last name. She keyed in the name anyway and hit 'Search'. Yes! There was just one Victor. His file contained details of his career with Rexco (accountant), how many years he'd been with them (forty), and something called 'risk factor'. This was rated as 'medium'. A visit to Minimerica three years previously was categorised as 'DL', which Rorie, benefiting from Lonnie's insider-knowledge, understood to represent 'Damage Limitation'. Underneath, success rating for this visit was listed as:

100%. Subject fully compliant.

Now that Rorie had Victor's surname, she tried a search on his daughter, Nina. Her details flashed up:

Risk Factor: high. Urgent therapy required. Subject prone to resistance, dangerous levels of independence. Dismissal no longer an option. Suggested duration of stay on Minimerica: three weeks.

Rorie gasped. It all reminded her far too much of Poker Bute Hall, the 'Anger Management Course' her friend Moll had been sent on, and how Moll had changed when she returned... Consulting the alphabetical list of visitors, Rorie now saw that every single one was either a past or present Rexco employee, or related to one. And somehow, when they returned to work, they were changed, in much the same way that Moll had been. The more Rorie thought about it, the more it appeared that Rexco was just like some giant grown-up version of Poker Bute Hall, full of robotic individuals without an independent thought between them.

Then a devastating thought occurred to her: were her parents among them? She quickly did a search for Arran Silk:

It was the same for Laura Silk; Rorie's parents were not here on Minimerica. She didn't know whether to be disappointed or relieved. But her mind was still full of questions: what *happened* to people on Minimerica? What made them so absurdly happy – far more so than could be expected from a visit to a theme park? And if Minimerica was such a big secret, which apparently it was, how come no one said anything about it when they got home? Rorie consulted the 'General' screen. As she did so, the 'Lonnie' part of her directed her first to the data relating to 'Atmospheric Levels'. There was all the usual information about cloud cover, wind direction, humidity...then she noticed more unusual data:

RX COMPOUND
Recommended level for conditions:
moderate, 450 – 600 parts per billion

Current level: 502 pp | IIIIIIIIIIIIIIIIIIII |

RX compound? What on earth was that?

Again, Lonnie's knowledge was able to fill in the

blanks. This was the cocktail of 'happy' chemicals Minimerica was pumping into the atmosphere. *So that's it!* thought Rorie. This explained a lot, not least the weird emotional ups and downs she'd been feeling each time she switched identity. And now here she was, sitting right at the central computer that controlled those levels. Straight away, she took it down to zero:

Current level: 0 ppb
```
┌─────────────────────────────────┐
│                                 │
└─────────────────────────────────┘
```

Then Rorie found more data, also in the atmospherics file:

CONCEALMENT
Fog Generator:
Recommended level for conditions: high
Current level:
```
┌─────────────────────────────────┐
│ ||||||||||||||||||||||||||||||| │
└─────────────────────────────────┘
```
Satellite deflector: last report,
Miss T 20/06/ – 100% effective.

Rorie was not at all surprised by this – she had suspected that the strange fog they had encountered was artificially generated – but she was delighted that she was now able to interfere with it. Again, she took the level down to zero.

There wasn't anything she could do about the satellite deflectors, though. Nor was there much she could do in the 'Dietary' section, which showed a long list of foods and which additives were in them. Apparently yesterday morning's pancakes had been full of mood enhancers.

Rorie searched for something else she could change, then hit upon something called 'Subliminals':

Frequency: every 30 seconds
Duration: 0.005 seconds

Thanks to the Lonnie factor, she understood that this referred to images and messages that appeared on screens all around Minimerica, so briefly that people absorbed the information without realising it. It had the effect of hypnotising them into believing only good things about Rexco. At first Rorie considered bringing this down to zero...but then she had a better idea. She *increased* it:

Frequency: every 30 seconds
Duration: 1.5 seconds

As far as she could tell, this now meant that these 'hidden' messages would be exposed for long enough each time for people to notice them.

Rorie sat back and allowed herself a satisfied little smile. She would have to stop soon...but first she would just look in on the 'Residents' of Minimerica, and find out who they were. After that, all she had to do was find a way to meddle with the lock on the computer-room door – the longer she could prevent anyone from getting in there and finding out what she'd been up to, the better...

Rorie had no idea what would happen next. How long would it be before the decreasing levels were noticed by somebody? She imagined that elsewhere in Minimerica there had to be people keeping an eye on these things... She would just have to wait. She removed Lonnie's slippers and lay back on the bed, looking forward to at least a bit of time just being herself. She toyed with a digital game until, little more than an hour later, she heard the front door slam. She jumped up and quickly grabbed the Elvis necklace, then waited anxiously by the door.

Thump, thump, thump, came the unmistakable sound of Elsie hurrying up the stairs. Then she flew into the room, wild-eyed. 'Rorie?'

'Elsie, what is it?'

'Well, we were just in Hollywood, when Lonnie's beeper went off...it's some emergency thing, she said.'

Rorie closed the door. 'Did she say what kind of emergency?'

'No, just that we had to get back as soon as possible.'

'OK, did you notice anything different...in the air, for example?'

Elsie shrugged. 'Not really...why?'

Rorie showed Elsie the Lonnie slippers. 'I got into the computer room,' she whispered. 'They've got stuff pumping into the air, stuff in the food...mood-altering chemicals. Then there's the fog...Lonnie controls it all, and I've interfered with it. Oh, and Mum and Dad aren't here, I checked. And those strange people – like that woman we saw in New York – there's loads of them apparently. They're ex-celebrities who nobody cares about any more, but who need to go on believing the public love them.'

'Oh yeah, Hollywood's full of them,' said Elsie.

'Anyway,' said Rorie, 'I have a plan for our escape...kind of. I really wanted to get away at night, but there isn't enough time...'

'How?'

Rorie pulled a small electronic device from her pocket. 'Lonnie doesn't know I have this. It starts the—'

Elsie's eyes widened. 'Shh!' she hissed, finger to mouth. She opened the door slightly, and they heard voices downstairs.

Rorie instinctively flattened herself against the wall behind the door. Taking a deep breath, she put on the Elvis necklace, realising it was only a matter of time before Lonnie sought her out.

'...Some sort of malfunction with the door,' Lonnie was saying, apparently to Max, who seemed to have just arrived. 'I don't understand it! I'm putting in the code, but it's not opening.'

Elsie shot a glance at Rorie, who, head swimming with the Elvis-change, managed a nod. Benefiting from Lonnies's know-how, she had been able to reset the code on the door; Lonnie would never guess the new one.

'...I have to get in there, Max!' said Lonnie. 'We need a technician – and quick.'

'I know,' said Max. 'This is hitting all over, from Liberty to Golden Gate...fog cover's dangerously low.'

Then their voices dropped, and the girls could make

out no more; Elsie closed the door. She looked at Rorie, alarmed – she was sliding down the wall. 'Rorie, what's the matter?'

'Nothing, it's just...these changes. They make me feel ill!' She closed her eyes and breathed deeply, waiting for the transformation to finish.

A moment later the door opened, and in walked Lonnie with Squint-Eyes and Pizza-Face. Rorie was in the final throes of her change. 'Celia, are you all right?' asked Lonnie.

'Oh, sure thing, Mrs Bix,' said Rorie, relieved at the depth of her voice, but alarmed at the sight of the guards. She did her best not to show her panic. 'Just, uh, finishing up some *exercises*.' She did a couple of press-ups against the wall, for effect, then shook out her arms; she felt good and strong now. 'Is everything all right?' she asked. 'Annabel says you got some emergency?'

Lonnie smiled briskly; a terse flash of teeth. 'We're experiencing a low-grade security alert situation, that's all. I'm sure it'll be cleared up in no time. Meanwhile, Norman here is going to be your chaperone for a while.'

Squint-Eyes stepped forward and sneered at Rorie.

'It's just for your safety,' added Lonnie. 'No need to be worried.'

But after Lonnie had left Squint-Eyes with them, Rorie heard her growling to Pizza-Face: 'When are those other guys gonna be here?' Pizza-Face assured her it would be as soon as possible, and she snapped, 'Well, get 'em to hurry up!'

Rorie knew Lonnie was no fool; she suspected her. And with more security men on their way, there was no time to lose. Rorie was pretty sure that right now there was no one guarding the *outside* of the building, since Squint-Eyes and Pizza-Face had been brought inside...which was itself quite a major inconvenience.

'C'mon then, *Elvis*, why dontcha sing for me,' goaded Squint-Eyes.

Rorie felt the loathing swell up inside her; to her shock, she felt the urge to punch him on the nose. She restrained herself, just grunting, 'I ain't in the mood.'

'Yeah,' added Elsie, aping Rorie's Elvis-accent. 'She *ain't* in the *mood*.'

'"She"?' taunted Squint-Eyes, turning to Elsie. '"*She*"? Ha! You wanna know what *she* is? A freak!'

Rorie felt the blood pulsing through her veins. She massaged her fists, cracking her knuckles.

'...A weirdo!' Squint-Eyes went on. 'A certifiable, one-hunnerd-per-cent – guh!' He didn't get to finish his sentence, because Rorie had punched him in the ear, with full-on manly strength. He reeled, stumbled and turned – just in time to receive another almighty punch in the face. No one was more surprised at this than Rorie, who glanced, wide-eyed, at her hands: such strength!

'Way to go, Rorie!' cried Elsie.

Squint-Eyes lumbered sideways, near the open wardrobe. Rorie gave him a good strong shove, slammed the door and locked him in. 'Ha!' she exclaimed, exhilarated. Then, retrieving Lonnie's slippers from under the bed, she put them on, and picked up the backpack. 'C'mon, Else, we're outta here.'

'But how... You gonna be Nikki Deeds now?'

'Uh-uh, no time... I'm a *fit* Elvis, maybe you noticed – two years' experience in the US army. Don't think Norman there' – she jerked her head in the direction of the wardrobe – 'was bargaining on that.'

Chapter 30
The Ex-Celebs

'Just *jump*. It's safe, I promise you!' hissed Rorie-as-Elvis-and-Lonnie.

Having escaped through the window to the rear of the mini White House's roof terrace, she had found to her great relief that she was right: so far, no outdoor guards. Ignoring, as best she could, the excruciating sensation as Elvis and Lonnie pulled bits of her in different directions, she braced herself for the climb down. The mini neoclassical colonnade was small enough that she was just able to shimmy down one of its columns – though she struggled to keep Lonnie's slippers on as she went. She had then rushed over to the pool where she retrieved the Bix children's enormous inflatable spaceship, and positioned it at the base of the colonnade.

But Elsie was reluctant to jump. 'Oo-oh!' she

wailed, trembling on the roof.

'C'mon!' urged Rorie, terrified that they might be seen at any moment. 'It'll be the softest landing. This thing is, like, a metre deep!'

'Oo-ooh!' cried Elsie, as she shut her eyes and flung herself down, landing with a *boof!* on the spaceship, then bouncing a couple of times before rolling to the ground. Rorie removed the Elvis-hair pendant and put it in her pocket; from now on she would need just Lonnie's expertise.

Together they ran past the pool, and on to the hangar that housed the Bix aeroplane. 'Rorie!' gasped Elsie. 'You're gonna fly a *plane*?'

'Yup,' said Rorie, trying not to sound nervous as she followed the Lonnie instructions in her head, and hurriedly circled the plane making checks. Feeling the Elvisness fall away from her, she stepped up and into the cockpit – no need for fingerprint or iris scans here, as Minimerica wasn't exactly awash with trained pilots eager to get away.

Elsie followed her. 'Rorie, are you sure—'

'Sh!' hissed Rorie, throwing Elsie the backpack. 'Get in the back and strap yourself in.' She took a deep breath, concentrating hard as she stared at the array of switches in front of her. The Rorie part of her was overwhelmed. For a moment she just sat there, nauseous with a combination of nerves and the biofuel-and-burning-dust smell. She needed to wait, anyway, for the last vestiges of Elvis to disappear, so that nothing came between her and Lonnie's aeronautical know-how. As the information began filtering through, she started flicking switches and adjusting levels. '*Rudder, throttle, carburettor,*' she muttered under her breath.

'But Rorie—'

'Shush, will you!' yelled Rorie, as she put on her headset. 'Here,' she said, handing another one to Elsie. 'You'll need this.' She pushed a button, and all the lights came on.

'OK, but don't you think they're gonna notice this?' Elsie blurted.

'Hmm, I wonder,' said Rorie sarcastically. 'Do you think *you'd* notice someone taking off in a plane in your backyard?'

'Oh yeah, definitely,' Elsie replied earnestly.

'The *idea*,' Rorie explained, 'is to get it into the air before they can do anything about it.'

'Aah, OK.'

Rorie pushed the electronic starter into its dock while pumping the throttle; the propeller cranked into action, and the plane sprang to life, vibrating loudly.

...And fly away so fast that they can't shoot us down, she thought anxiously. *Would* they shoot down their own plane? Perhaps not. All the same, Rorie was terrified. She tried not to be – fifty per cent of her was, after all, an experienced pilot – but it was no use; the other fifty per cent that was still Rorie had mostly to do with her character and emotions, and she had no control over that.

You can do this, she told herself. She had sailed a boat through a storm, hadn't she? And that was without any help from another guise. This ought to be easier, if anything, with Lonnie's slippers. *So do it!* Excited and terrified in equal measure, she pushed the throttle forward, and the plane began to move. But as it gathered speed, a warning signal went off, drawing attention to an obstruction on the runway.

'Oh no...'

'What?' asked Elsie.

'There's...*people* on the runway,' explained Rorie, now able to see the obstruction for herself.

'Oh my God, there's loads of them.'

'What people? Officials?'

'No. They're...' The crowd was coming towards them, clothes flapping in the draught from the propeller; they were clearly intent on keeping the plane from taking off. 'What's that they're carrying? Placards? Oh, I don't believe it! Elsie, they're the ex-celebs I was telling you about!'

'Oh, the pretend-famous people?'

'Yes. And they're...they're *protesting*. Oh boy... *I* did this.'

'What do you mean?'

'I've messed with their heads all over again. By shutting down all that feel-good stuff in the air, I've made them suddenly realise that they're just a sad old bunch of has-beens. Now they're furious!'

The ex-celebs were advancing. Rorie had the impression that they had all turned into caricatures of their former selves. Many of them were, Rorie couldn't help noticing, XL-sized: a product of so much happiness-enhanced food, combined with the adulation they carried on getting regardless of how they actually looked. They lolloped along like creatures not meant for land-dwelling, dimpled blubber rippling as it spilt out the sides of their tight, hopelessly out-of-date clothes. Others had become addicted to cosmetic surgery, their skin stretched thin and eerily translucent over their jutting bones, startled-fish faces clown-like with lipstick and eyeshadow. Their placards read 'GIVE US BACK OUR LIVES!' and 'I'M A CELEBRITY, GET ME A COMEBACK!'.

Rorie was paralysed, consumed with a mixture of panic, guilt and revulsion.

'What we gonna do?' asked Elsie.

'I...I...' Defeated, Rorie brought the plane to a standstill. 'Oh, just look at them! I never thought this would happen...I should never have...'

'It's not your fault,' said Elsie. 'You didn't make them the way they are.'

'Well, no, but...OK, I'm going to have to explain I'm not the one they're after – maybe then they'll get out of the way.' She glanced nervously over at the house; she thought she saw some movement, but couldn't be sure. There was very little time. She leant over, unlocked the door and slid it aside, prompting a great whoosh of air and noise. The ex-celebs surged forwards.

'You have to let us through!' Rorie yelled. 'We're nothing to do with all this!'

'Oh, but you're *everything* to do with it,' asserted the foremost ex-celeb, whose stick-frame and bug-eyed sunglasses gave her an insect-like appearance.

'No, you don't understand!' cried Rorie. 'I'm not

who you think I am. I'm Lonnie's...sister.'

'Well, *I* am Ira de Monde,' announced the ex-celeb raspingly, removing her glasses with a flourish as if expecting all around to fall at her feet at this revelation. 'And I *insist*—'

'I don't care who you are!' interrupted Rorie, her panic now trampling over her manners. 'I told you, I'm not Lonnie. Now let me go!' She reached for the door handle and began to pull it shut, but a greater force was pulling it the other way. In another moment, a large, purple-clad bottom had wedged itself in.

'OK, everybody!' announced the owner of the bottom. 'I don't know about you, but even if this was Lonnie, she ain't the one I'm most mad at right now, anyhow.'

Right, screamed Rorie's head. *So get your butt out and let me go!*

But the Bottom had other ideas. 'What about Nolita Newbuck, huh? Strikes me, this is a golden opportunity to hitch ourselves a ride back to London and have it out with her. *She's* the one who shot me to fame, then dumped me out here. How about you guys?'

Rorie closed her eyes in disbelief. *This cannot be happening, not now!*

'Nolita, yes!' came the cries from the crowd, as their anger focused itself roundly on its target. Nolita, Nolita: *she* was the one.

'Take us to her. Now!' demanded the owner of the bottom, turning around.

'Are we being hijacked?' asked Elsie.

'No!' yelled Rorie. 'She hasn't got any weapons.'

Elsie surveyed their intruder. 'She *has* got a very big bum,' she pointed out, ominously.

'You can't do this!' Rorie shrieked at the ex-celeb.

'Just you watch, honey,' said the woman, as she began helping her grateful cohorts up onto the plane. 'You gotta take us, or else these guys aren't moving from the runway, see?'

Chapter 31
High Flyers

'Rorie! They're coming after us!' cried Elsie, looking back towards the mini White House.

'Who is?' demanded the fat ex-celeb.

'Never mind!' cried Rorie. 'All right, I'll take you! I'll do anything – just get in. No, hey! We can only fit seven...quickly, *please*...'

'Thanks!' said the ex-celeb, beaming at her as if touched by Rorie's generosity. 'I'm Gula, pleased to meetcha!' she added, offering her hand. Rorie just glared. 'Oh, suit yourself,' said Gula, then turned to the others who were still on the ground. 'Out of the way, OK?' she yelled. 'I promise we'll do everything we can to help all of us. Solidarity!' And she gave the crowd a fisted salute.

'And if they believe *that*, they'll believe anything,' muttered Ira.

Rorie flicked a switch, and the door slid shut. Gula clambered noisily into the back. 'OK, here we go!'

Rorie increased the throttle. The ex-celebs still on the ground quickly dispersed. As the plane began to roar, gathering speed along the runway, Rorie could see on her digital display the shapes of vehicles chasing her – and gaining speed.

More throttle. Faster, faster...a car was now alongside the plane. What was more, Rorie was running out of runway space. She would have to take off now...the Lonnie part of her knew this was risky – it was too soon, she hadn't gathered enough momentum. Yet the risk of *not* taking off was so much greater...

Slam. Rorie pitched the elevator and the plane lurched upwards. It wobbled and dipped, and the Lonnie part of her brain directed her to the stick control between her knees. *Left side up, right side down*, said the voice in her head, which knew how the device was controlling the flaps on the wings. *Rudder to the right!* it demanded forcefully, as the plane veered leftwards, prompting cries of terror from the ex-celebs in the back.

'Quiet!' yelled Rorie-as-Lonnie, tense as a coiled spring. 'I must concentrate. I need silence!'

The ex-celebs quietened down for a moment – but not for long.

'Uh...just how experienced *are* you at flying a plane?' asked Gula nervously, fiddling with a large black brooch on the front of her blouse.

'Oh, this is the first time!' said Elsie cheerfully.

'*Aauuargh!* Let me out of here!' cried Ira.

'Oh, I think I'm going to be sick!' wailed another.

'It's not true!' yelled Rorie. The momentary distraction caused the plane to lurch again, dipping sharply. Rorie struggled to regain control.

'OK, what I meant was,' Elsie added hurriedly, 'she's *really* experienced...but only half of her is.'

'Oh. My. God,' groaned Ira, massaging her temples.

'What do you mean, only half of her is?' demanded Gula.

'No, I din't mean to say that,' said Elsie. 'It's just...don't worry. She can fly. I fink.'

'Urrgh...'

Rorie took the plane higher: 1,400 metres, 1,500 metres. Finally, when they reached 1,524 metres, the plane began to steady. Minimerica, no longer shrouded in fog, disappeared beneath them. *We did it!* thought Rorie. *We got away*. As the aircraft steadied, she felt the tension ease in her shoulders.

But there was still the worry of where they were headed now...

As if reading her thoughts, Elsie said, 'Rorie, can we just go home now? I mean *home* home. I'm tired.' Her voice wobbled, as if she were going to cry.

Home. How desperately Rorie wanted to go home as well! Back to her own bed, with her own parents in the next room... 'We can't, Elsie, you know that.'

'Well, where are we going to go, then? New York?'

'Uh-uh. Not in this little thing, Elsie, don't start on that one again. Even if we do need to go there, it won't be in this plane.'

Gula, who in spite of the aircraft noise was obviously listening intently, leant forward. 'Ahem, you're *going* to Nolita Newbuck's place, London.'

'Oh, I'm taking you to London all right,' Rorie called back. 'But you can find your own way to Nolita's.'

'Hey! Do you *realise* who you're talking to?' retorted Gula, forgetting the 'ex' part of her celebrity status.

Rorie shut her up with a deliberate dip of the elevator, causing more shrieks from the back.

'Just be quiet, Gula,' said Ira. 'And let's get there in one piece.'

The plane steadied again. Leaving the ex-celebs to mutter amongst themselves, Elsie said, 'Well, we'd better go to Inspector Dixon, then. He'll sort us out.'

'No way!' said Rorie. 'I'm not going to him...we're going to find Mum and Dad ourselves. That's what we agreed, remember?'

'Yes, but, I mean, where are we going to stay?'

'I don't know! I'll figure something out, OK?'

They sat in silence for a moment or two. The plane rumbled on contentedly. Rorie could feel her bones aching from all the transformations. She thought of the crisp, warm sheets of her bed at Nolita's, the yielding softness of its pillows...how she wished she could go there! But those days were well and truly over now. She thought about Nolita's blank stare, her vague reply, '*Oh, it's some sort of scientific organisation, right?*' when asked about Rexco. Knowing what she knew now, Rorie's anger at Nolita returned tenfold. If she was pretending she had nothing to do with Rexco, then what else was she hiding? Was it possible that she did know something about what had happened to their parents after all? Rorie's head was filling up with fog; she no longer knew what to think about anybody. But perhaps if she were to confront Nolita squarely about it...

'All right, here's what we do,' she said at last. 'We go with them to Nolita's.'

'But you said—'

'Not to *return* to her, Elsie! To find out once and for all just how much she knows. I've nothing to hide any more. I don't care if she knows that I snooped in her computer files. Look, we've got a mystery to solve, and after what we've found out about Minimerica, this seems the next logical step. And maybe – *maybe* – having this lot on our side' – she jerked her head in the direction of the ex-celebs – 'might help us get that information out of her.'

'But Nolita doesn't *know* what's happened to Mum and Dad,' insisted Elsie.

'You don't know that! Look, remember what she said? "Just get on with your lives and don't expect them to come back"? Well, at the time I thought she meant, you know, don't wish your life away, 'cause that's the way she put it. But now…*now* it feels like that could mean, "Hey, stop being such a nuisance, and leave well alone". Look, she's connected to Rexco, and Rexco created Minimerica – you've got to wonder what she's capable of!'

Elsie thought about it, staring blankly ahead of her. No matter how hard she tried, she couldn't believe that Nolita was capable of such evil. But Elsie certainly wasn't going to object to returning to her; she had her own reasons for wanting to go there. Deep down, she desperately wanted to believe in the fantasy that Nolita was some sort of fairy-godmother figure. She had even had dreams in which she was exactly that, literally waving a magic wand – *twinkle twinkle!* – and making Mum and Dad appear again. Elsie had gone along with her sister's plan of leaving Nolita just because Rorie had been so determined, and because she herself had thought that finding Mum and Dad was just a matter of a quick boat ride to New York. But now, hope rose in her heart again; maybe they had got Nolita all wrong. She was quite sure the ex-celebs had, too. Maybe they just weren't much good, and they were looking for someone else to blame. *No, none of this is Nolita's fault*, Elsie told herself. *Nolita's on* our *side...*

'OK, we go to Nolita's.'

Chapter 32
The Spider Tattoo

'May I help you?' said the tiny woman, smiling sweetly as she opened the door to Nolita's house.

Rorie had never seen her before in her life. 'Um...oh, I was expecting Cammy...'

'She left,' explained the woman. 'I've taken her place. I have a number for her if you want...?'

'No, it's OK,' said Rorie. 'It's Nolita we're here to see.' She had finally caved in and told the ex-celebs how it was that they knew Nolita. The one thing she hadn't been able to explain was the change in her appearance, now that she was no longer in her Lonnie guise. When Gula had quizzed her about it, she had suggested all sorts of possible explanations, from a 'trick of the light' to the effects of altitude.

The maid blinked prettily. 'And your name is...?'

'Rorie...and Elsie.'

The maid just smiled blankly. 'I'm sorry, did you say you had an appointment?'

'It's *us*,' said Elsie. 'Rorie and Elsie!'

'I'm very sorry, but—'

'Now look here,' barked Ira impatiently, pushing herself forward. 'We demand to see Miss Newbuck immediately!'

'Oh, we're *going* to!' added Gula, shoving the maid out of the way. The poor dainty creature was helpless to resist as the angry mob of ex-celebs forced their way in.

Bringing up the rear, Rorie glanced anxiously at the maid. 'I'm sorry, I...'

Elsie grabbed her hand and pulled her along with the rest of them. Rorie quickly moved to the head of the group. 'This way,' she told them, as she led them up the stairs and into Nolita's bedroom suite.

Nolita was sitting on a couch, zipping up her boots. With her was Misty, the reflexologist, who was quietly preparing to leave. Nolita jumped up. 'What the heck...how did you get in here?' She reached for her Shel, but Ira got it from the table first.

'We're your *friends*, Nolita – remember?' challenged Ira, holding the Shel away from Nolita. 'No need to call security.'

'Yes, remember me?' added Gula, stepping forward. 'Long time no see, eh, Nolita?'

'Give me back my Shel!' demanded Nolita. 'You're no friends of mine, and you've no right to be here. I've never seen you before in my entire life! Is this some kinda joke?'

'Joke? Oh, you might think it's a joke, Nolita,' hissed Gula. 'But *we* don't think it's very funny, being dumped out there in "Beverly Hills", cast aside like…like last week's fashions!' This set off the others, all protesting loudly.

'Quiet!' commanded Nolita. 'OK, now listen to me: I. Don't. Know. *Any* of you. Understand?'

The seething anger on Gula's face gave way to simpering desperation. 'Nolita, it's me, Gula! C'mon!'

'What part of "*I don't know you*" do you not understand?' asked Nolita furiously. She turned to the reflexologist. 'Misty, call security!'

'Wait!' said Rorie, stepping forward with Elsie. 'Nolita, you know us.'

Nolita's face was blank – not a glimmer of recognition. 'No, I don't.'

Rorie was flabbergasted. 'I…' She and Elsie exchanged disbelieving glances. 'But it's *us*…Rorie and Elsie…' She trailed off, suddenly aware of how

286

much like the others she sounded.

'Nolita!' exclaimed Elsie desperately.

But there was not the slightest sign that Nolita had ever set eyes on them before this moment. It couldn't have been faked. Now her anger was giving way to confusion. Her face twitched, and she looked away, her hand to her head. 'Misty, what's happening with the security guys?' She sat down, sighing. 'Oh, I don't feel too good. I think I need to reboot again.'

'I was thinking the same thing,' said Misty. 'Don't worry, we can start over.' Rorie noticed she didn't appear to have called security yet.

'Reboot?' said Gula. 'What's she talking about?'

'You've got her all stressed out,' said Misty. 'So she needs a foot massage and a fresh pair of boots. It's very calming, energising; you should try it some time.'

'Listen, lady—'

Misty calmly put her finger to her lips; a slight, quiet gesture, yet somehow it instantly silenced Gula.

Rorie strode forward, trembling with fury. 'No! That can wait,' she snapped. 'We've waited long enough for answers, now tell us, Nolita: what happened to our parents?'

Nolita's green eyes looked unfocused. 'I don't know...who are they?'

'Never mind, Nolita, relax,' said Misty as she knelt down, unzipped Nolita's boots, and went to work on her feet. Rorie had never noticed it before, but there was a small tattoo on Nolita's right ankle, which seemed to be of a spider. 'She can't answer you right now,' said Misty. All the tension in Nolita's body dissolved, and the creases in her brow melted away. 'Just be patient,' Misty went on soothingly, 'and the answers will come.'

Rorie was still seething with frustration. 'What does that *mean*?'

Misty turned and hushed her. Rorie instantly felt suspended, as if time were holding its breath. Nobody moved: to do so felt as if it might break something fragile. *Be patient*, said the words in her head, *and the answers will come*. And she wanted those answers so very badly...

Misty went on murmuring to Nolita in gentle, rhythmic tones. Rorie could just make out the odd phrase here and there: '...moving on...new and wonderful things...not dwell on what's gone...' Soon Nolita was sound asleep.

Misty stood up, turned and smiled that enigmatic smile of hers. Rorie was reminded of how doll-like her face was, its broad, porcelain expanse punctured with small, black-rimmed eyes and a tiny red mouth. Her long, thick black hair was tightly woven into glossy coiled locks and tied back with a grey scarf. 'There's nothing to worry about,' she assured them. 'Nolita's fine, she's just tired. And so are you, I think...very, very tired.' A large screen on Nolita's wall flickered to life, and the image of a sort of tunnel of water appeared, accompanied by watery sound effects.

'This is crazy,' retorted Ira dismissively. 'NOLITAAA!'

Nolita didn't stir.

'She won't respond,' said Misty, stepping forward. Her expression was one of utmost serenity. Somehow, Rorie found herself irresistibly drawn to her. Misty reached out and touched Ira gently on the shoulder. 'But it's OK – you can wait here...just wait. There's no rush, everything's fine. The answers will come.' Rorie remembered when she'd last seen Nolita being 'rebooted', when she was stuck on ideas for her 'Next Big Thing'. And the answers had come, as they always seemed to do. *Yes...perhaps I need rebooting too*, thought Rorie. She certainly felt jammed up with information. The idea of wiping the slate clean, starting again, now seemed immensely appealing. Then all would become clear: she would know exactly how to find Mum and Dad...

Still murmuring, Misty touched Gula, who promptly sank down on the huge, semi-circular couch. She moved among the group, repeating the words, 'No rush...everything's fine...' while water whooshed gently in the background. The ex-celebs gratefully reclined. 'There's plenty of time,' said Misty, smiling gently.

Now she laid a hand on Rorie's shoulder, and something warm like liquid silk seemed to radiate into her bloodstream. Suddenly Rorie was overwhelmed with tiredness; her legs folded beneath her and she sank down into the soft white seat. She guessed the exhaustion of the transformations and the stress of the flight were catching up with her... *Reboot, wipe the slate clean...the answers will come...*

Now Elsie; down she went.

Rorie closed her eyes. Too many transformations. She needed to wash them away, start afresh. She felt the thoughts untangle themselves in expanding loops, like loosening yarn. Rushing water merged with Elvis songs... Max Bix appeared: *Never thought I believed in carnations...Lonnie makes the best chicken pot pie, don't you, hon?...* Lonnie: *I sure do...* Slippers, hallway, computer imagery... *RX COMPOUND...*

current level: 502 ppb... Satellite deflector: last report, Miss T 20/06/ – 100% effective. Miss T? Somehow that had registered, but at the time Rorie had thought nothing of it. Miss T...why did that seem to mean something?

The answers will come...

Miss T: the sound of it glinted, hard and shiny like a needle piercing the yielding threads of her thoughts. Rorie felt a sudden jolt of anxiety. She was falling, falling into dense woolly softness, but she strained to stay alert, to respond to the sharpness. Her eyelids were heavy as lead, but she forced them half open.

'*When you wake, you will wonder where you are, but you will not be afraid,*' Misty was saying...Misty! Miss T...were they one and the same? Over there was Nolita, still asleep. The spider tattoo, previously black, was now glowing red like hot coals...

Oh no, Rorie realised at last. *This is very, very wrong!*

Chapter 33
The Scrunchy

Resist, resist, Rorie told herself. How could she not have realised they were all being hypnotised? Did that mean that Nolita was being hypnotised as well? Was 'Misty' controlling her? If she really was the 'Miss T' from Lonnie's computer, then that might well be the case. Here could be the very person they were after – the one behind Minimerica, so clearly a very important Rexco person...*she* should know what happened to Mum and Dad. How very clever to disguise herself as a humble therapist, while pulling the strings from behind the scenes...

The tattoo glowed: what *was* that?

Everyone else was asleep. Misty moved from one to another, checking them, still talking. Then she turned. Rorie quickly shut her eyes.

She felt the closeness now. She felt the touch of

Misty's hand on her brow, was lulled by the soft voice. The warm liquid silk flowed into her again and she was sinking, sinking... No! *Resist*... It was harder than ever, and before she knew what was happening, she felt something cold and hard, first her right wrist, then her left. It felt alarmingly like handcuffs. Panicked, Rorie desperately wanted to fight back, but found herself unable to move a muscle. Misty removed her shoes, then repeated the exercise with her ankles. Rorie was trapped.

Her heart pounded so hard, she felt sure Misty would hear it. After a moment, she risked a peek out of one eye; Misty now had her back to her. Rorie turned to Elsie, slumped beside her, blissfully unconscious of it all. But she wasn't handcuffed – in fact, none of the others were; Misty must have sensed that Rorie was not responding well.

Elsie's hair was tied loosely with her favourite scrunchy...this gave Rorie an idea. She nudged closer and carefully lifted her locked-together hands, hooked her finger into the scrunchy and slid it off. Then she resumed her pose, eyes shut, the scrunchy enclosed in the palm of her hand, and awaited the transformation.

Still those soothing words came, still the falling water...Rorie used every morsel of energy to fight it.

There was no room in her head for any thoughts about the weirdness of turning into her little sister – staying awake was all. She heard a sound like a short metallic buzz, followed by a dull *clunk*... Rorie risked another peek, and saw Misty bending over Ira, a steel gun-like device in her hand. Ira now sported a glowing red spider on her ankle, just like Nolita's.

Rorie quickly shut her eyes again. She would *have* to wait for the changes, she had no choice...but for how long? It was happening already, she could feel herself shrinking...but not enough yet. Would it stop before she was slender enough to slip out of the restraints? Would she stay awake long enough, even if it didn't?

The answer soon came with a sensation of renewal, a refreshing of the mind. She knew the transformations could have this effect; that they could do so even when her subject was under hypnosis was a revelation.

Bzzz–clunk. There goes another one...

Now Rorie's clothing felt looser...and so did the restraints. She tucked the big toe of her right foot inside the left ankle-restraint and tried to yank it down, but it wouldn't go beyond her heel...

She waited some more.

Bzzz–clunk.

Rorie tugged again, and this time just managed to slip the restraint over her foot, which must have shrunk by about three sizes. Quick as she could, she wriggled her hands free and, dropping the scrunchy as she went, threw herself right at Misty's legs, buckling them instantly. Misty fell to the floor, dropping the gun device; Rorie grabbed it and ran to the other side of the room.

Misty stood up, still remarkably calm. One or two of the ex-celebs stirred, until Misty lulled them back into a trance, telling them that sudden or loud noises would not trouble them. Still softly spoken, she addressed Rorie. 'It won't do you any good, you know. Security will be along any minute. Somehow I don't see you fighting off seven strong, hefty men.'

'Tell me what you've done with my mum and dad!' Rorie yelled.

Misty didn't flinch. 'What *I've* done? What on earth are you talking about?'

'Oh, don't pretend you don't know! You're controlling Nolita, *Miss T.* What does the "T" stand for?'

'My name is *Misty*. I've no idea who this "Miss T" is that you've confused me with, or what you think she's up to, but I can assure you that my work with Nolita is nothing but positive and healing. She endures a great deal of stress, and I help her with that.'

'*Help* her? Is that what you call it? With this thing?' She waved the gun.

Misty gave a pitiful half-smile. 'Every job involves electronic technology these days. Mine is no different.'

'You *are* Miss T, I know it! It all fits. I know about your connection to Minimerica!'

Misty frowned. 'My connection to *what*?'

'To Minimerica! Don't pretend you don't know what I'm talking about. I've seen your name on the computer. You're part of the whole thing!'

Misty's wide, pale face took on a look of deep concern. 'Child, you are suffering from paranoia. What *is* this "Minimerica"?'

'You know perfectly well what it is,' insisted Rorie, grateful for the growing she was now doing as the Elsie-guise faded – Misty certainly knew how to cut people down to size. 'They tried to kill us!'

'Who are "they"?'

'*Minimerica!* They shot down our boat!' Rorie noted the barely concealed surprise on Misty's face as she registered the changes in Rorie's appearance. But she no longer cared who knew about that.

'I know nothing of this place. Perhaps you were breaching security,' said Misty. 'Or, more likely, you are completely deluded. I can help you with that.'

'I'm not falling for any of that nonsense!' snapped Rorie. '*What about my parents?*'

Misty held firm. 'I haven't the slightest idea what you're talking about.'

'You do, I know you do!'

'Oh dear,' yawned Misty, as she went and knelt beside Nolita. 'Child, you believe what you like. Why don't you go to the police? Oh, but I think you've committed a number of crimes by now, haven't you? That boat you mentioned – where did that come from?'

'That was—'

'And how was it you got here from this "Minimerica" place?'

'Ah, now that—'

'Then there's trespassing,' added Misty as she massaged Nolita's ankle; the spider glowed. 'And fraud – I know about your talent for, ah, *changing* – though I have to admit this is the first time I've seen it first hand. Quite impressive, I must say. And so useful for getting away with crimes – until someone's onto

297

you, of course. Even at your age, there's only so much you can get away with.'

'I—'

'*Alternatively*,' Misty now moved from one ex-celeb to another, rousing them. 'You could patch up your differences with Nolita, and you will be protected.'

Six burly security guards burst in. 'Ah, hello,' said Misty. 'Would one of you hand me that, please?' she asked politely, indicating the gun device Rorie had clamped to her chest. One of the men nodded and duly headed over to her, as Misty continued, 'Now, Rorie. Nolita will remember you when she wakes up. But she won't remember anything about your disappearance, and no one will charge you with anything.'

Rorie dodged the guard and hurled the device across the room, smashing it to pieces.

'Tut-tut-tut, even that,' added Misty, as another guard picked up the pieces. 'So, which is it to be?'

'You must be out of your mind,' Rorie spat, now held firm by the first guard. 'I don't care what sort of trouble I get into. What I've done is nothing compared to the crimes you've committed!'

Meanwhile, Elsie and Gula slept on. The rest of the ex-celebs, however, began to stir, looking very confused. 'What's going on?' asked Ira. 'Where am I?'

'You've been hypnotised!' cried Rorie. 'And what's more, you've got some sort of implant controlling you now, just like Nolita. *She* did it,' she added, nodding angrily at Misty. 'Just look at your ankle!'

Ira looked. Her face brightened. 'Ah yes, I remember now. I was having a tattoo done. So painless! I must have drifted off. It's lovely!'

Misty shot Rorie a sharp, superior look. 'You were saying, Rorie?'

The five other ex-celebs who Misty had roused now sat up and examined their own ankles; they too made admiring noises, happily chattering among themselves.

Rorie couldn't believe it. She wriggled helplessly in the guard's firm grip, yelling, 'They're not just tattoos. They've got microchips inside, controlling your minds!'

The ex-celebs stared at her quizzically.

'Don't worry about her,' said Misty. 'She's a little confused; I'm going to explain everything to her in a moment. Meanwhile, I wanted to introduce you to these gentlemen.' She beckoned to the guards, except the one who was restraining Rorie. They stepped forward. 'They're here to escort you home.'

The ageing women all gazed up admiringly at the

well-toned torsos of the youthful men, clad in tight-fitting T-shirts. This was all the distraction they needed. 'Ooh, thank you!' they cooed. One by one, they stood up, took the arm of one of the men, and drifted happily out.

Rorie stared after them in disbelief. 'They'll just send you back!' she cried. 'I *rescued* you from there, for heaven's sake!'

Misty regarded her pitifully. 'They don't *care*, Rorie.'

Rorie glanced at Gula, who was still asleep. 'What about her, then? Ha! You didn't get to inject that thing in her, did you?'

'It doesn't matter,' said Misty, in that soothing voice of hers. Yes, it was *very* soothing, like sinking into a warm, fragrant bath... 'People will do what they want, Rorie,' her voice trickled on. 'Poor child, you feel you have to manage everything...I *understand*. You're trying to compensate for something terrible that happened, over which you had no control...'

Rorie felt herself melting. 'No!' she cried, shaking her head. 'You're doing it again; I *won't* give in. Elsie! Wake up!'

'All in good time,' said Misty. 'Don't worry. Everything will be fine, you'll see.' She passed a hand over Nolita's forehead, gently rousing her. 'Hi, Nolita.'

Nolita stretched and looked around. 'Mm, hi. Aah...hey, Rorie, how's it going?' Just as Misty had said, it was as if she had never been away.

'Nolita, you have a visitor,' said Misty, passing a hand over Gula's forehead; she too woke up.

Nolita stood up. 'Gula! This is incredible. I was just dreaming of you!'

Gula looked surprised and delighted. 'You...you mean you remember me?'

'It's so great to see you!' Nolita went on. 'I was going to call you; I got a great makeover plan that'll kick-start your career, for sure!'

Gula positively glowed. 'Really? Oh wow, this is amazing! Really?'

While they carried on with their chatter, Misty turned to Rorie with a look that seemed to say, '*There. See how I sorted everything out?*' But seeing Rorie's look of defiance, she reached into her case. Pulling out a hypodermic needle, she came towards her.

'What are you doing?' asked Rorie, instinctively struggling in the grip of the guard, even though she knew it was useless.

Nolita looked up. 'What's going on?'

'Don't worry, Nolita,' said Misty, turning to her.

'It's *nothing to worry about*.'

Nolita's face slackened momentarily in response. 'Ah. OK.' Then she turned to Gula and resumed her chatter, oblivious. Those words, 'nothing to worry about', were clearly ones which Nolita had been programmed to respond to obediently.

Rorie felt her breath shorten as Misty came closer and closer. 'It's going to be fine,' murmured Misty gently.

Chapter 34
The Brooch

Once that needle goes into me, thought Rorie, *it's over.*

Misty drew nearer...

The only part of Rorie that was not confined right now was her legs – perhaps she could remember how to do those athletic Nikki Deeds moves? A *very* high kick might do it. But was she supple enough?

Do it! You have to try.

Now Misty reached for Rorie's arm, still clamped to her side by the security man. It would take all the propulsion of a kangaroo-leap to knock that thing out of Misty's hand...but she just *had* to try... She wriggled and yelled, forcing Misty to wait while her captor tried to secure her more tightly. Rorie lowered herself, to aid the propulsion upwards.

I am Nikki Deeds, she told herself. Concentrate: mind over matter, like in Chinchilla's fabulosity lessons. *I am* Nikki Deeds...

It happened as if by magic. Right leg, up and over, far higher than she had dared imagine possible. 'Aah!' cried Misty, as the needle flew out of her hand onto the hardwood floor.

'Elsie, wake up!' cried Rorie, but it was no use; loud noises alone wouldn't rouse her. But the right *words* just might... 'The boat's going to explode!' she yelled. 'Get ofmmm—' Her voice was muffled as the security man's hand covered her mouth.

But it had worked – Elsie opened her eyes.

Misty picked up the needle; it was broken. Nolita came over. 'Misty, hon, what *is* going on here? I'm trying to have a conversation with Gula!'

'I told you, Nolita, it's *nothing to worry about*,' insisted Misty once more.

There was the blank stare, the glassy eyes. 'Oh. OK, Misty!' said Nolita, almost childlike. She half turned, then paused. 'All the same, this is aggravating,' she added, as Rorie went on wriggling and making muffled cries.

'Let go of her!' cried Elsie, still somewhat dazed.

'Yes, Mark, let her go,' agreed Nolita. 'She'll behave herself if I tell her to.'

Rorie felt herself released.

'Nolita—' began Misty, but Nolita held up her hand.

'It's OK, Misty, it's nothing to worry about. Hey, Rorie, sit with us...c'mon!' She beckoned, smiling encouragingly.

Rorie followed, falteringly. Misty watched her intently. Rorie could almost hear her mind ticking over, as she tried to work out what to do next to take control of the situation. She herself was wondering the same thing...

'Why's that Mark man here, anyway?' asked Elsie, indignantly. She tried to stand, then slumped back down.

'Good question,' said Nolita. 'Mark, you can go now.'

'No, Nolita,' said Misty firmly, staring into her eyes. '*Mark must stay.*'

'Oh, all right,' said Nolita.

'Well, he better leave off my sister!' remarked Elsie.

'It's OK, hon, he will,' Nolita assured her. 'OK, I got some work to do on tomorrow's schedule, Rorie,' she said as they sat down. 'Now, where did I put my Shel?'

Gula, oblivious, still yammered on about ideas for her big comeback. She fiddled with her brooch, which seemed to be a habit of hers.

'Sure, honey...uh-huh,' muttered Nolita, but she was distracted, still hunting around for the Shel. 'Hell, where is it?'

At that moment, Rorie spotted the Shel on the floor near Elsie, peeking out from under a cushion; it must have slid from Ira's hand as she fell under the hypnosis, then been concealed by the falling cushion.

Rorie went and sat next to Elsie, and hid the Shel with her feet. Aware that Misty was watching, she leant back and made as if she were handing Elsie something. 'I'm pretending to pass you the Shel,' she whispered, though her voice was easily masked by Gula's. 'Take it to the other end of the room, and look all secretive.'

Elsie obliged by looking furtive and pretending to put the 'object' behind her back. Meanwhile, Rorie acted as if she were helping Nolita look for the Shel. Now Elsie stood up and stepped around the side of the couch, never turning around, her hands behind her back. Misty and Mark moved in on her – and, crucially, away from Rorie.

With Nolita and Gula still searching elsewhere, Rorie seized the moment: she grabbed the Shel, and located the listing for 'Dixon'...no time for talk or text, she just hit the emergency alert button. '*Best way to reach me,*' she remembered him telling Nolita...though there was no way of checking that the alert had actually worked. She could only hope and pray it had...

At the other end of the room, Misty had descended upon Elsie. 'Show me!' she demanded.

'What?' said Elsie, spreading her hands. 'I haven't got anything!'

'Oh look, here it is,' said Rorie, pretending to have just found the Shel on the floor.

'Hey, thanks,' said Nolita. She took it and began consulting it.

'Nolita, let me see that,' demanded Misty. Rorie felt her skin prickle, as she sensed the shift in Misty's suspicion: no doubt she wanted to check the call log. And if she did, she would see what Rorie had done and cancel the emergency alert.

But, to Rorie's relief, Nolita shot her an irritated glance. 'Misty, you're being weird; stop it. Maybe you should go home now. And girls, you go on to bed.'

But Misty didn't leave, and nor did Rorie and Elsie; there was no way they were going to give Misty and Mark the chance to pounce. Misty hovered, lying in wait like a spider in her web, ready to suck their brains clear like a pair of soap bubbles.

Rorie was determined to stay close to Nolita for protection, no matter what. But then Nolita suggested to Gula that they take a walk in the garden. 'I know it's late, but...hey, I feel so energised now! I'll put the lights on.'

'Great!' said Gula, fiddling with her brooch.

Rorie jumped up. 'Can we come?'

'No!' said Nolita sharply. 'This is business; and I've just told you two to go to bed.' She peered at Gula's brooch. 'You got a problem with that thing?'

Gula flushed. 'Oh, it's just, uh...the clasp. It's digging in.'

Nolita reached over. 'Let me see.'

Gula twisted away from her. 'Oh, I got it...it's OK now. Let's go.'

Rorie could tell that Gula was lying, and her curiosity was aroused. Gula was *constantly* fiddling with that brooch. Why? And why should she not want Nolita to touch it? Suddenly, Rorie thought of a way she might buy a little time until Dixon arrived. *If he was going to arrive...*

Gula made as if to get up, but the bulk of her torso gave way to the force of gravity, and she slumped down again, laughing. Perfect: Rorie seized her chance. She came forward as if to assist her...and, as she did so, ripped the brooch off Gula's blouse and ran across the room with it.

'Hey! Gimme that back!' cried Gula.

'Uh-uh!' Rorie briefly inspected the brooch.

'Rorie, what's gotten *into* you?' demanded Nolita, as she got up and strode over to her. She was swiftly followed by Misty and Mark; Gula lumbered behind. Elsie threw herself in their path, which enabled Rorie to dodge them long enough to get almost as far as the door, but Mark got there first so she quickly diverted, throwing herself under the couch. Again, she tried to study the brooch, but it was too dark...then she felt a strong hand grip her ankle, after which she heard Mark howl – had Elsie bitten him or something? – and the hand released.

Rorie slid along the floor to the other side of the couch, where Misty was standing; turning on her side, Rorie raised her knees to her chest and shoved her feet at Misty's, toppling her. She scrambled out from under the couch and raced to the door, but that was soon blocked by Gula, until Elsie dive-bombed into her belly – *oof!* – doubling her over. Rorie dashed out onto the landing and dived down the stairs, but got only halfway before Mark grabbed hold of her by her left arm. Rorie tugged and tugged, but he now had a firm grip on her. In her right hand was the brooch; once again, she looked closely at it, and now at last she could see what it really was...

She tugged again, but Mark was stronger and now his other, bleeding hand was on her arm too and pulling, pulling...

Rorie sensed something move down below in her peripheral vision; she turned and saw that the front door was open, and all of a sudden, there was Inspector Dixon.

'Catch!' cried Rorie, throwing him the brooch. 'It's a camera!'

Chapter 35
New Nolita

2.30 am, just over twenty-four hours later

'Hey, Rorie, wake up!'

Rorie felt her shoulder being nudged. She heard the words, but she was so sleepy, the meaning of them didn't quite register. She groaned.

'Rorie, *wake up.*'

It sounded like Nolita's voice. But how could it be? She was still in police custody, wasn't she? Rorie opened her eyes and peered into the gloom. The bedside light came on. Yes, it really was Nolita – though she looked different. Softer…no make-up, Rorie realised. No fancy hairdo.

Rorie felt a stab of dread or excitement; she wasn't sure which. After twenty-four hours of languishing at the house in the care of the maid, Gula, and a woman police officer, she was still no closer to knowing how she really felt about Nolita now.

Rorie pulled herself up, blinking. Elsie was already awake. 'What time is it?' Rorie asked Nolita. 'How come you're...'

'I was released earlier today,' explained Nolita. 'Then I had the chip removed, and some corrective therapy... Don't worry, they're still holding Misty,' she added quickly. 'And I'm having nothing more to do with her. Or Nolita Newbuck, for that matter. Girls, I'm finished with it all. I invented Nolita, just like I invented Gula and Iva Pasquale and all the rest of them. Then she got out of control, and I couldn't even see what was happening. So get up, we're leaving.'

'Leaving?' said Elsie. 'Where we going?'

'Somewhere secret. Fresh start. Gula's coming too. Come on, get dressed.'

'But –'

'Elsie, I'm sorry to do this to you, hon, but I have to, can't you see? I have to disappear. And I wouldn't just leave you behind. Besides, think about it – we'll be able to do our detective work from there!'

'*Our* detective work?' said Rorie. 'You mean, you'll help us look for our parents? But I thought you said—'

'Nolita *Newbuck* said,' corrected Nolita. 'I'm just

plain Nolita now, with no ties to anything. The new Nolita, if you like. And the new Nolita can see that Rexco are capable of anything. Come along, there are bags for your clothes over there. I'll be back for you in fifteen minutes.'

And she left. Rorie and Elsie stared at the door for some time after she'd gone, still taking it all in.

A warm bubble of hope rose in Rorie's belly. Could this really be happening? It seemed almost too good to be true. For twenty-four hours, she and Elsie had had the awful uncertainty of wondering who would take care of them next. And on and on, one change after another...

For Rorie, it had certainly dampened her feelings of vindication and triumph over Misty – although the relief of that had been enormous. Dixon had, of course, been most concerned by the images from Gula's camera. Gula had become obsessed with turning her life into one long movie, and the scenes she captured meant that at last, Dixon didn't think Rorie was completely loopy. There was Nolita's blank stare as she failed to recognise Rorie and Elsie, saying she'd never seen them before in her life. Then the sequence showing Misty taking hold of Ira's leg and holding the chipgun to it, *bzz-clunk*, followed by the sound of further *bzz-clunks* off camera, and all that that implied.

What was more, intelligence reports had begun to make waves in government circles: they showed images taken from a container ship of what appeared to be some sort of island where there wasn't supposed to be one. These had begun to filter down into the police force...thus, when Dixon took statements from Rorie and Gula about Minimerica, he took them seriously.

Now wide awake, Rorie pulled on her slants. So many transformations, she thought; and this time, for once, she wasn't the one who was changing. How must it feel for Nolita? Unlike Rorie's transformations, this one was meant to be permanent: a rebooting to end them all.

Though there was, Rorie realised, a kind of permanence to the changes she'd been through herself. It was as if she were a passport, embellished with an ever increasing number of visa stamps – or a tree, acquiring another ring through its middle for every year that passes. Each transformation made a small permanent change, little by little turning her into a different, wiser, more able individual. She thought back to the person she'd been at Poker Bute Hall, and almost didn't recognise her.

'I don't know if I'm going to get everything in there,' said Elsie forlornly, standing beside her crammed wardrobe as she stared at the rather compact bag.

Rorie rolled her eyes. 'God, Elsie, do you never think of *anything* except clothes?'

Elsie shrugged. 'Not really.'

'Well, they won't all fit, so you'd better just pick a few. Honestly, Else, it's not that important.' Rorie set about packing her own things. For her part, she didn't care if she had nothing but slants and tops, same for every day. Although...there were those items that had belonged to other people – her transformation kit. She knew they were important. She picked up the small box that held the Elvis-hair pendant, and opened it. All of a sudden, she felt nauseous and short of breath. The sensation came back to her of how it had felt to be consumed with Elvisness – like drowning. It had been the same with the Lonnie slippers – the transformations seemed to be growing more all-consuming each time. Could she ever face another one?

'Why aren't you packing?' asked Elsie.

Rorie snapped the box shut. 'I am. It's just...' She

hesitated. 'I am.' Yes, she would bring these things along. Because whatever else they may have achieved with Minimerica, with Misty...the biggest challenge still lay ahead of them – that of finding their parents. The pieces of the puzzle may be falling into place, but the crucial ones were still missing. And to find those, Rorie was going to need all the help she could get.

Don't miss...

The final thrilling instalment of

trilogy

t i g e r – l i l y

Rorie and Elsie are on the run – again! But now the
enemy is bigger and stronger than ever before.
The mission to rescue their parents will take them on a
wild and dangerous journey, deep into the nerve centre
of the corporate machine that is robbing more and more
people of their identities...

Can they unlock the powerful secrets at its heart and
save their parents before it's too late?